Divide
The
Child

"The King said, 'Bring me a
sword . . . Cut the living
child in two and give half to
one and half to the other.'"
I Kings 3:24,25

Karen Robbins

AUTHOR:	Karen Robbins
FRONT COVER DESIGN:	Karen Robbins
	H. Donald Kroitzsh
LAYOUT & DESIGN:	H. Donald Kroitzsh

This book is a work of fiction. Names, characters, places, and incidences are either a product of the author's imagination or are used fictitiously. Any resemblance to actual persons, living or dead, events, or locales is coincidental.

For information or orders contact:
Five Corners Publications, Ltd., 5052 Route 100
Plymouth, VT 05056, USA. Phone—800-972-3868

Visit Karen Robbins' Website at:
http://people.delphi.com/karenrobbins/

Scripture taken from the *Holy Bible, New International Version,* ©1973, 1978, 1984 by International Bible Society. Used by permission of Zondervan Publishing House.

Printed in Canada

Published by:
Five Corners Publications, Ltd.
5052 Route 100
Plymouth, Vermont 05056   USA

Divide The Child
ISBN: 1-886699-18-6

God has blessed me with a wonderful family. The deepest love and respect goes to my husband, Bob, who patiently loves me through all of life's trials. I am grateful for my children who encourage me, Ron, Rob, Andy (Drew), Cheryl, and Don, and for my daughter-in-law, Lori, who courageously plodded through my rough drafts and had faith in me.

Many friends have helped along the way. Michele Burke, my writing buddy, kept me on track. Sheryl Arden just kept loving me. Beth Lucius gave me a wonderful idea to complicate my plot. Toni Marsh helped to refine the legal aspects of the story and made my business law class exciting.

My church family has been so supportive and encouraging, especially seeing me through difficult times. God has truly given them the gift of loving.

And, without my loving Father, whose footprints are always in the sand even when mine aren't, nothing would be possible.

One

The Yellow Mustang

You're paranoid, Julie told herself, as she walked along with Kathy happily skipping beside her. It couldn't be the same car you saw yesterday. The yellow Mustang convertible continued to shadow them on their way home from Kathy's school. How many yellow Mustang convertibles had a W on the hood ornament? For that matter, Julie couldn't recall if Mustangs even had hood ornaments. She had never paid much attention to cars. Something about this one though, unnerved her.

She shrugged. It was probably someone in the neighborhood coming home from work too. Maybe someone from the hospital who works the same shift I do, Julie thought. It would be nice to arrange a ride home when the weather got snowy. The five blocks to Kathy's school and then the three blocks home could be a pretty miserable trek if they had a hard winter.

"Let's sit on the porch swing a few minutes and enjoy this wonderful crisp fall air," Julie said as they approached the front walk. "You can tell me all about what happened in school today."

The porch steps creaked slightly under the weight of mother and daughter. The endearing sounds of an old home were comforting. What would have been considered old and dilapidated to most, appeared as character and charm to Julie. She saw potential in everything. A house with potential meant a house that could hold all the love and warmth they could fill it with. The neighborhood wasn't terribly friendly but that was fine. Julie and Rick were content to stay mostly to themselves. It was safer that way. The one exception was Mrs. Burke. Mrs. Burke was a kindly grandmother who had taken to Kathy. She lived two houses from the Sierras and had offered to stay with Kathy each morning for the fifteen minutes it took Rick to drive Julie to work and return. Mrs. Burke would walk her dog to the Sierras house, tie him outside and grab a cup of Julie's coffee while she waited for Rick to return. She was very reliable and Julie was truly grateful for her.

Kathy started the swing with a push of her feet and ignoring, the grating sound of rusty metal chains, began her litany of the day's events with all the enthusiasm of a first grader who hasn't learned that kids are not supposed to enjoy school. Her dimples deepened each time she grinned and her brown eyes sparkled with flecks of gold. She radiated love and happiness and Julie absorbed all she could from this child whose life had become so precious to her.

Julie and Rick had struggled with the dilemma of finishing their education before starting a family. They had waited until Julie's nurse's training was well along and Rick was nearing the completion of his medical degree. When they ceremoniously tossed Julie's birth control pills into the trash can and began to look for the signs of pregnancy, their faith in God was tested and stretched as month after month they were disappointed.

Then came Kathy. Beautiful, pink, button-nosed Kathy. Julie was sure this was God's answer and her assumption was reinforced each time she touched those soft auburn curls or heard the giggles that erupted from Kathy's throat as she and Rick tumbled on the floor.

"Yes, Lord," Julie prayed silently, "I am truly grateful for Kathy. Help me to be a good mother and, especially, help me to teach her of your love for us."

". . .and the teacher put a sticker on it," Kathy said looking at Julie who was staring down the street. "Mommy, did you hear me?"

Something yellow had caught Julie's attention. It was the Mustang again, slowly passing in front of the house. Julie strained to identify the driver. It was definitely a woman and, as she turned toward them, Julie had the nagging feeling that she knew that face from somewhere. Was it from the hospital?

"Time to get dinner started," Julie said shaking off the uneasiness. "We're having spaghetti tonight."

"Susgeddy!" Kathy squealed as she hurried up the stairs to change clothes.

"Spa—get—tee," Julie corrected. She almost hated teaching Kathy the proper pronunciation of some of her words. The innocence of a child's vocabulary would be lost soon enough. She disliked the rate at which Kathy was growing. Too soon she wouldn't be their little girl any more.

Rick brushed back the sandy colored lock of hair that always fell across Julie's forehead by the end of the day and kissed the top of her head as she snuggled next to him on the couch after dinner.

"That was pretty good 'susgeddy' you made, woman," he said.

"Spa—get—tee," Julie said, drawing it out for emphasis. Her brown eyes glistened as she peered into Rick's deep blue eyes. Julie knew the sun on the ocean could not shimmer as tenderly as the love reflected there. "How am I ever going to teach Kathy if you keep that up?"

"Just be sure you teach her how to make your terrific sauce. She won't have to know how to say it then," Rick teased, playfully pulling her hair. He kissed her lightly.

Julie smiled as she looked from Rick to Kathy who was in her familiar TV position on the floor, stomach flat on the rug and chin resting in the palms of her hands. Could anything be more peaceful and right than this moment? All her dreams of marriage and motherhood had come true. It had been worth all the sacrifices.

"The air smelled so good today walking home," Julie said, sighing. "It reminded me of apple cider—sweet and tart. The sun was warm but the air was cool."

"It won't stay that way much longer," Rick commented. "I wish we could find some way of getting you a car. It's bad enough you have to work, but I can't even supply transportation for you," Rick replied.

"But I want to work. I enjoy nursing as much as I enjoy being a wife and mother. The walk is good for me and it gives Kathy and me some special time together."

"Well, if you insist. But the first opportunity we have to get you some wheels, we're going to do it. When the weather begins to remind you of frozen marshmallows, it's not going to be as pleasant a walk home. One more large drugstore account and I should have enough commission to pay off my student loan and get you something reliable."

The thought went through Rick's mind that if they hadn't had to move to a new town, he would have been in private practice by now and they wouldn't be struggling. It had always been Rick's dream to be a doctor. His father had wanted Rick to pursue his talent as a golfer, something Rick's father couldn't do because of his accident. He tried instilling his own pro-golf dream on Rick but in the end, just before his death, he had joked that at least Rick would out play the rest of the physicians on the course on Wednesdays. But now, Rick's dream too had gone by the wayside. Quickly he put those thoughts behind him. Kathy had brought such joy into their lives. . .well, he wouldn't change anything. He couldn't now anyway.

"Getting you a car also means we wouldn't have to leave Kathy in the mornings while I take you to work," Rick added.

Rick did have a point there, Julie thought. That was the only bad time of the day. It was still dark in the morning when Julie left for work and Rick insisted on driving her there. Kathy was usually asleep, and Julie hated to impose on Mrs. Burke.

"Bedtime, sweetie," Julie said to Kathy. "Go up and put on your pjs. Daddy and I will be up to tuck you in."

Kathy made a face but obediently got up and headed for her bedroom. A few minutes later, Rick and Julie, arm in arm, made their nightly climb up the stairs for Kathy's bedtime rituals.

". . .and bless Mommy and Daddy. . .and Herman, too," Kathy added, finishing her prayer with a hearty, "Amen!"

"Is Herman a new friend?" Rick asked. This was the first time she had mentioned anyone named Herman.

"No, silly. Herman lives at the zoo. He's a HIPMOPATUS. We read about him in our story hour today. Someday, our class is going to visit him. He can hold his breath a long time and stay under water and. . ."

"Oh," Rick responded trying to contain a chuckle, "you mean a hippopotamus. Herman the hippopotamus."

"Yeah! A HIPAMOTAPUS. Anyway, he can. . ."

That's enough, young lady," Julie said. "You're stalling and it's time you were asleep. Good night."

"G'night," Kathy said flipping over and snuggling up to her love worn Pound Puppy, Wilbur.

Julie went to Kathy's window and drew the curtains closed. She shuddered involuntarily. As she turned to join Rick in the hallway, she questioned whether she had really noticed a yellow car across the street or had she just imagined it?

"Have I told you today that I love you?" Rick asked drawing her close. She warmed to his gentle touch.

"Yes, but you can tell me again."

"I love you."

Julie felt secure in his arms as they embraced. Rick was strong physically as well as spiritually, and she drew much of her own strength from. His reddish brown hair almost matched the color of Kathy's and they shared a common dimple. With those features added to Julie's brown eyes, no one doubted that Kathy was their biological child.

They were the perfect family. So perfect that it scared Julie.

The driver of the yellow Mustang watched as the last light went out in the house and then slowly edged the car away from the curb and down the street a block before putting on the lights. It rounded the corner and disappeared into the night.

Sebrena Warner maneuvered her yellow Mustang into the garage next to her husband's blue Cadillac. She would have enjoyed driving a yellow Porsche more that the Mustang Wynne had bought for her but, with Wynne's politics, they were careful to buy American-made cars in order to encourage the unions to support him. The garage door closed quietly at the push of the button on her remote control.

Wynne would probably be waiting up for her. Sebrena straightened her skirt, smoothed her dark hair a bit and took a deep breath before entering the house. Wynne would want to know all about her evening. She had gone over and over her story as she drove home from the east side of town. It would pass. It had to. He couldn't know what she was doing—not just yet.

"Well how was your night out with the girls?" Wynne asked barely looking in her direction. He was engrossed with the late newscast. Sebrena was used to losing him to the news programs and papers and the local voters when they were out in public. She didn't mind. She knew it was important to him and she enjoyed the attention his political aspirations brought her also. After all, this year the state senate and maybe, in a few years, she could be picking out a nice second home in a chic Washington, D.C. suburb.

She sat next to Wynne on the sofa and scratched his back lightly as he hunched forward listening to the reports of another large factory moving out of state. For a man who sat behind a desk most of the day, he was in remarkable shape. Early mornings spent in their workout room paid off in building stamina as well as the muscles that she felt ripple under her touch. He let out a soft low hum of appreciation but didn't look at her until the commercial break.

"Well," he said, his hazel eyes penetrating her veneer. Did he suspect something?

"Well, what?"

"You didn't answer my question."

"I'm surprised you noticed," she said using a teasing lilt to her voice to cover her nervousness.

"I notice everything about you," he said pulling her down into his lap and kissing her hard and long. "I missed you."

"I've only been out for one evening. Surely you kept busy licking campaign envelopes for me. They do need to go out tomorrow."

"All taken care of, boss lady. But you still didn't tell me how your evening went."

Sebrena had hoped she had thrown him off the track. Obviously she was going to have to give her well rehearsed story.

"We had a great time catching up on what's happened since college. But, you know," she paused for effect, "Gracie and Nell just don't seem to have a lot in common with me anymore. They are settled into middle class ruts. I like where I am now. It's exciting being with you and campaigning."

"No regrets?" Wynne asked. She had gone through a lot to be with him. A messy divorce followed by a child custody suit that barely seemed fair. In the end Sebrena had lost permanent custody of her two children.. She had made some regrettable mistakes and her ex-husband had been able to use them and magnify them enough to cause the court to rule against her.

All that was behind now and, while Sebrena did miss her children once in a while, Wynne was just as glad that the two of them did not have that responsibility. Sebrena was free to travel and be at his side through whatever campaigns were ahead. Maybe after his political career was more established, they could think about a family.

"My only regret is having to share you with so many others," Sebrena answered, "especially all those female voters." Her statement was not all in jest, Wynne's intense eyes, his dark wavy hair graying at the temples and the body he kept in such good shape was extremely attractive. She wondered how many women would be voting for his physical appearance rather than his political views.

Still, he had waited until he was 35 to marry and part of that time he had spent waiting for her to be free. That gave her a feeling of confidence in their relationship.

When the newscast ended, Sebrena led Wynne to the bedroom unbuttoning her blouse seductively with one hand as she pulled him by his loosened tie with the other.

"What are you up to?" he asked grinning, as if he didn't know. She was an exciting vivacious woman. Her hair, long and silky, framed the fair skin of a soft face sculptured only by cheekbones that gave her a classic look and eyes set deep enough to invite you to wander into them. She was unpredictable, a bit too impulsive, but she made life explode with promise. That's why he had been willing to wait for her and chance any stigma that might still be attached to marrying a divorcee. They had been married almost four years now and the thrill of being with her hadn't diminished.

"I wouldn't want this evening to be a total waste. Besides," she added, kissing his ear, "you deserve a reward for licking all those envelopes, don't you?"

And, I want you in a good frame of mind for tomorrow, she thought. She had waited long enough. Tomorrow she would do it.

The next morning, Sebrena watched as Wynne turned the corner in his Caddy on his way to his early brainstorming session at the Anderson and Warner Ad Agency suite. Wynne always laughed at Bob's name being first even though Wynne had started the agency. He claimed he took Bob on as a partner to get top billing in the phone directory. With Wynne's successful lifestyle, Sebrena had everything she wanted—well, almost. And she would take care of that today.

Grabbing her sweater and keys on her way out, Sebrena hustled to her car. As long as there was no traffic jam, she should be able to make it just in time. After all, she'd been through enough dry runs now to know. Quickly she dialed the phone.

"Hello," said Mrs. Burke.

"Mrs. Burke, this is Julie," said Sebrena.

"Julie, is anything wrong? You sound a little strange."

"No, Mrs. Burke. Maybe I'm just getting a cold. I meant to call you last night but I forgot. We have a friend coming today to take Kathy on a special outing. You won't need to come over this morning."

"Oh what fun for Kathy. You have a good day, Julie."

"Thanks," Sebrena said hanging up quickly and running out to the car. The yellow Mustang flew out of the driveway and headed for the east-west freeway.

Two

The Abduction

The alarm woke Julie with a start. She had been dreaming about the Mustang. In the dream, she knew the driver. She shivered. Just a dream, she told herself as she swung her legs out from under the covers.

Julie tossed on her chenille robe and whipped the brush through her tousled sandy brown hair. After plugging in her curling iron, she went down to the kitchen to start the coffee. She pulled out the coffee grinder and her special bag of gourmet flavored beans. It was a small luxury she allowed herself and, to keep the expense down, she mixed the freshly ground cinnamon-nut flavored coffee with an equal amount of canned coffee grounds. She enjoyed these few moments alone at the kitchen table with her open Bible and devotional guide, taking in the wonderful smell of brewing coffee along with some words of inspiration to carry her through her day.

This morning she was reading Proverbs 16:16. "How much better to get wisdom than gold, to choose understanding rather than silver." Solomon had chosen to ask for wisdom and, amidst all his wealth, he still treasured wisdom over all the rest.

Oh to have the gift of wisdom Solomon had, Julie thought. With wisdom you could make all the right choices all the time. Knowing what to do, what direction to take, would certainly erase the worry and doubt from their lives. Most of all, she would be sure her decision about Kathy had been right.

Rick's heavy footsteps across the bedroom floor jiggled the ceiling light slightly. Julie took a moment for a quick prayer and then set about getting the cereal bowls out. She poured steaming black coffee into a large mug and sipped the luscious brew with her eyes closed. She was glad they were a cereal for breakfast family. The thought of having to cook a big breakfast and then clean up before work was not at all appealing.

The early morning sun began to brighten the sky. The days were noticeably getting shorter. Just a few weeks ago, the sun would have peeked into the kitchen by now and added to the room's cheerfulness. The ruffled peach curtains softly framed the view through the window. The violets on the sill were still in full bloom. They certainly loved that window. She hoped they would not mind moving away from the window when the weather got colder. Julie loved their small Victorian house. It needed some repairing and remodeling but it had felt like home the moment they entered. She knew the kitchen would become her favorite place. A kitchen was the heart of a home. It radiated love and each new day was born there. This kitchen with its old worn hardwood floor and painted wooden cabinets was well used. A lot of love had passed through here. Julie could feel it. Maybe someday they would have enough money to make an offer on the house. For now, they would have to be content to rent.

The wonderful smell of his after-shave announced Rick"s presence before Julie felt arms around her waist and a nose nuzzling the back of her neck.

"Mmm, good morning," Julie said as she turned to put her arms around Rick's neck inhaling his wonderful smell. He pulled her close.

"Good morning. Looks like another one of your apple cider days." He squeezed her tightly for a moment. "This is nice but we'd better get moving or you're going to be late for work."

"Maybe I could call in sick and we could spend the morning trying to diagnose my problem," Julie teased.

"Sure. But you'd probably fall asleep and I'd never get to finish the examination."

Grinning, he sat down to his bowl of Cheerios .

"Now you'll never know," Julie taunted him. She poured his coffee and then exited the kitchen with her own cup, humming a little chorus and looking forward to the day ahead.

After she was dressed, Julie peeked in at Kathy's sleeping form. Wilbur, her Pound Puppy, was hanging precariously over the edge of the bed. Julie tucked him back in carefully so as not to wake Kathy. She quietly backed out of the room and then dashed down to Rick who was starting the car.

"Where's Mrs. Burke?" Julie asked. Mrs. Burke was usually headed up the drive by the time they were pulling out.

"I haven't seen her yet. I'm sure she'll be here in a minute." Rick slipped the car into reverse and slowly started down the drive.

"There she is," Julie said as she saw Mrs. Burke coming out the door of her house with her frisky dalmation excitedly waiting for her owner to lock the door. Julie waved and Mrs. Burke nodded back with a smile.

The traffic was a little heavy but they managed to arrive on time. As Rick circled the hospital parking area to drop Julie off, she looked for the yellow Mustang. If it was someone from the hospital, Julie reasoned, she could get a ride and then Rick wouldn't feel pressured to buy her a car. But Julie's real reason for wanting to find the Mustang, if she were honest, was to know who the driver was and release the gnawing uneasiness she felt.

No luck. There were a couple of Mustangs in the parking lot but no yellow convertible. Maybe she changes shifts, Julie told herself.

"Don't forget to pick up the milk for Kathy's cereal," she said as she opened the car door when Rick stopped in front of the outpatient entrance.

"One cow, coming up!" Rick waved and drove off in the direction of the little corner store.

Julie's thoughts began to center on her patients and the day before her as the large double doors swung open and she entered the hospital corridor.

Sebrena parked the Mustang in the driveway of the Sierra's small home. Pitiful little box, she thought as she hustled to the side entrance. She knew she had to move quickly. She had only ten minutes at best. She pulled her Nieman Marcus credit card out of her pocket. Thank goodness they couldn't afford decent locks, she thought. This would be a lot more difficult if they had the sophisticated security system that Wynne had put into their home. She tried the doorknob and found that it was open. Her credit card had been a useful key before, but, just as she thought, they left the door unlocked for old Mrs. Burke. She entered and headed straight for Kathy's room.

Kathy was sitting up in bed playing with Wilbur when Sebrena appeared in the doorway. Both of them were startled. Sebrena had not expected Kathy to be awake.

"Hello, Kathy," Sebrena said softly.

"Hi! Who are you? Where's Mrs. Burke?"

"Mrs. Burke isn't feeling well today. I'm a friend of your mommy and daddy. My name is Sebrena. Daddy took Mommy to work and they said that I could take you to the zoo today." Sebrena thought her heart was going to burst through her rib cage it was pounding so hard.

"The zoo? Really?!" Kathy was obviously enthusiastic.

"Yes, but we have to hurry if we're going to watch the animals have breakfast. Let's get your clothes and you can dress in the car."

"Can we see the HIPAMOTAPUS? I like the zoo. Will we see the monkeys?" Kathy continued to chatter as she opened a drawer to gather her jeans and a shirt.

Sebrena let out a low sigh of relief. This was easier than she had anticipated. The zoo had been the right key to Kathy's compliance. She glanced at her watch. She had three minutes at best before Rick Sierra would be back. She tried to hurry Kathy along.

"Where are your shoes?" Kathy crawled under her bed and came up with one sneaker.

"I can't find the other one," she said. "It's not under here."

Sebrena tensed. What would she do if she were caught in the house? She thought of sending Kathy to delay Rick at the side door with a question about the zoo while she slipped out the front. No, that wouldn't do, she had parked the car in the drive. She'd better just get Kathy out of here now, shoe or no shoe!

Two more minutes. She was wasting precious time. She knelt down to help Kathy search for the other sneaker. It wasn't in any logical place like the closet.

"Where did you take your shoes off last night?" Sebrena asked the little chatterbox.

"Right here on the bed," she said straightening and patting the disheveled mess on top of the bed.

Sebrena looked at the jumble of stuffed animals on the bed and wondered how Kathy slept with all the lumps. She began moving the Disney stuffed collection, the dolls and the rest of the menagerie.

One more minute! There, under a wrinkled bulldog was the lost sneaker. She added it to the pile of clothes in her arm and grabbed Kathy by the hand. "Let's hurry! We're late already!"

"Waaait!" Kathy wailed making Sebrena's heart stop. "Wilbur!" She turned grabbed the Pound Puppy by the neck. "O.K. We can go now."

The two quickly hopped down the steps. Aerobics had nothing on the way this activity was affecting her cardiovascular system, Sebrena thought. Reaching the car, she quickly deposited Kathy on the passenger's side, threw the clothes in her lap and picked the keys from the side pocket of her purse as she rounded the front of the car to the driver's side. She was shaking so badly that the keys fell to the floor when she slid behind the wheel. She fumbled under her feet for a moment to retrieve them.

"What's the matter?" Kathy asked as she slipped her shirt over her head.

"I'm just too excited about the zoo, I guess." Taking a deep breath, she made her movements more deliberate to avoid any more delays from clumsiness. Any second now, Sebrena thought, his car is going to pull in behind me. She could feel every blood vessel within her pulsating.

She started the car and began to back out of the driveway. There were cars coming from both directions. Sebrena was on the verge of panic. There had never been any traffic before. She paid close attention to be sure the Sierra's blue Chevy was not among them.

With relief she pulled into the street and headed for the corner. As she stopped at the intersection, she noticed the Chevy, turn signal blinking, coming down the road to her right. Quickly she put her hand under her open purse and upended it, spilling lipsticks, pens and loose change onto the floor beneath Kathy's feet.

"Oh, dear," Sebrena said. "Can you get that quickly before it all rolls under the seat?"

"O.K." Kathy said. She had responded automatically by ducking down to reach things as they began to fall. Her head was out of sight as the yellow Mustang crossed the path of the blue Chevy stopped at the intersection.

Julie should be driving a nice car like that, Rick thought as he waited for the yellow convertible to clear the intersection. He turned the corner, keeping one hand on the milk carton to steady it. Yes sir, an apple cider day. The sun was tinting the sky. Rick was whistling as he passed Mrs. Burke walking back to her house. Strange, he thought. She usually waits for me. Maybe she has a busy day today.

"Kathy," Rick called from the bottom of the stairs. "Rise and shine. I'm pouring your cereal." He returned to the kitchen and assembled the bowl, spoon, box of cereal and the milk. Mrs. Burke's usual coffee cup was missing. She hadn't even taken time to have coffee, he wondered. All was ready for the little princess' entrance. Where was she?

"Kathy?" he called again one foot on the bottom step. "Come out, come out, wherever you are." He began to climb the steps. It was awfully quiet. Even if she were playing a trick, by now he would have heard a muffled giggle. She must really be sound asleep.

Looking in the open door of her bedroom, he couldn't be sure if she was in the middle of all the lumps in the bed or not. He crossed the room and began poking at the various shapes. Nothing moved or giggled or, for that matter, felt warm. Nope, she wasn't in there.

"O.K., honey, we have to get going. You'll be late for school and I'll be late for work, and we'll both be in trouble. I'll close my eyes and count to three and you can surprise me. One. . .Two. . .Two and a half. . .Three!" He opened his eyes and whirled around. Nothing. This is getting eerie, he thought, and fought off an icy chill.

She's got to be somewhere else in the house and playing games with me. Is this some kind of surprise she cooked up with Mrs. Burke? Systematically, he began checking every room. Panic did not begin to creep in until he returned from the basement and realized there was nowhere else in the house to check.

"Kathy, this is not fun any more," he yelled. "Let's go. You'll be late for school."

She was gone. Just gone. The house was empty. No sound but the lonely ticking of the hall clock. Rick returned to the kitchen and frantically searched for Mrs. Burke's number posted near the phone with all the emergency numbers. When he found it, it took him two tries to dial it correctly because his hands were shaking so badly.

"Come on. Come on. Answer." Rick chanted. He tried to remember if he saw Kathy with Mrs. Burke. No, that was something he would have noticed. It was just the lady and her dog.

"Hello," Mrs. Burke finally answered.

"Mrs. Burke, this is Rick Sierra. Did you leave Kathy alone this morning before I got home?" He hated the accusatory tone in his voice. "I can't find her any where in the house."

"Oh dear, didn't Julie tell you that your friend was taking her for the day?" Mrs. Burke sounded a little upset. She was reeling from the tone of Rick's voice.

"Friend? What friend?"

"Julie called me early this morning. Gracious, I had barely gotten out of bed. She told me she didn't need me to stay with Kathy this morning because there was a friend coming to take her for the day. I don't think I dreamt it. Goodness, I hope not. Oh my."

"It's O.K., Mrs. Burke. Perhaps there's just been some kind of miscommunication. Let me call Julie." He barely said good-bye before he was dialing the hospital.

Julie poured herself a cup of wonderful deep black coffee. Normally one would expect hospital coffee to be thick, syrupy, and bitter. But the nurses on the sixth floor had gotten together and decided to purchase some specialty coffees. They were protective of their coffee pot. If someone from another floor headed for it, they were reminded that they had to pay their quarter to the coffee kitty. And there, next to the pot, was a black ceramic kitty, partially filled with silver, that had once been a planter abandoned by a patient. Word was spreading though, and it looked like they might have to insist that other floors get their own coffee conglomerates started or they would be making coffee for the whole hospital.

The patients under her care had put in a good night and seemed to be doing well. Julie planned to take care of the discharge papers for a patient while she had her coffee and then start setting up medications while Carrie watched the desk. She and Carrie worked well together and were becoming good friends as well as co-workers.

She went into the little office behind the floor desk and carefully copied the information requested on the discharge sheet from the patient's chart. The patient, Helen Belemonte, was a pleasant black woman who had been brought into emergency the day before because she was having a miscarriage. Actually the doctors always referred to it as an abortion, delivering an aborted fetus, but Julie didn't like the sound of that. The term miscarriage at least let people know that it was not the mother's choice to end the pregnancy. Julie felt sorry for her. She had looked drawn and very depressed this morning.

If only I could have some time to talk with her before she leaves, Julie thought. Maybe there would be a way to reassure her of God's love. But, then, so often she found that patients did not like to hear about a loving God when the emotional wounds were fresh.

She had mentioned her concern to the gynecologist in the hallway outside the patient's room. Mrs. Belemonte was a judge, Julie had been told. She was well educated and would survive the "slight setback" quite well. Julie knew education had nothing to do with the disappointment of not having a child or losing one. At least she would have the opportunity to wish her well when she took her the discharge slip.

"Julie," Carrie called in to her from the desk. "Rick's on the phone. Says it's really important."

Julie's heart began to pound. Rick never called her at work. She picked up the extension.

"Honey, something's wrong." Rick's shaky voice was enough to tell her it was terribly wrong. "I can't find Kathy anywhere."

"What?!" A twinge of fear knotted inside of Julie's throat and she fought to stay calm.

"I thought she was playing a game and hiding from me, but I've searched the whole house and. . ." he fought to control his voice.

"Where's Mrs. Burke?" Julie cut in.

"She was really weird. Said you'd called her this morning to say she didn't need to come...that a friend was going to take Kathy for the day."

"I did no such thing!" Julie shouted into the phone.

"Do you suppose when Mrs. Burke didn't show up that Kathy decided to head for school on her own?"

"It's a possibility. You call the school and I'll walk home and see if I find her on the way."

"Julie, if she's not at the school we need to call the police."

"I know. I know," said Julie, resigned to the fact that Kathy's safety outweighed any consequences incurred by calling the authorities. "I'm leaving right now. Call the school." Julie's breath was coming faster. Her mind began clicking off what she needed to do.

"Carrie, can you get someone to fill in for me quickly? I have an emergency at home. I have to leave immediately," she said when she saw Carrie at the door looking concerned.

"Sure," Carrie said, "What's wrong? Is there anything I can do?"

"Kathy's missing. Just find someone to fill in. I have to get home," Julie said grabbing her purse and coat. She should wait she thought, but Carrie would be able to handle things until someone came up from another floor. It wasn't like this was ICU.

The elevator took forever. "Should have taken the steps," she berated herself tapping one foot impatiently. She half ran, half walked through the hospital corridors. As Julie doubled her pace home, her eyes kept sweeping the yards and alleys. *Please, God, let her be safe. Just let her be safe.*

"Roosevelt Elementary, Mrs. Penney speaking." The principal's voice was so calm. For a moment it confused Rick. She should sound worried at least. But, reason told him, she didn't know yet.

"Mrs. Penney, Rick Sierra. I'm trying not to panic here, but I think Kathy may have taken it upon herself to walk to school alone this morning. Can you tell me if she's there?"

"The early arrivals wait in the cafeteria until the teachers are in the classrooms, Mr. Sierra. Let me check. I'll just be a moment."

One very long and empty moment later she was back. "I'm sorry Mr. Sierra, but Kathy isn't with the other children and no one else saw her on their way here. If she does come in, I'll get right back to you. In the mean time, maybe you need to notify the police. I don't want to worry you, but if she did start to school on her own. . .well, they can be on the lookout. Maybe she made a wrong turn. Call me when you find her."

A weak thanks crossed his lips. The police. It was the only option he had. Terror was beginning to fill him. Anguish could not fully describe the painful feeling that was beginning to overwhelm him. He couldn't take time to analyze it. He realized in that moment that his whole life had changed. At any given time of the day, we all carry pictures in our heads of the places we know our loved ones to be. He could picture Julie making her way home, searching for Kathy, but there was no picture in his head of Kathy. Nothing to reassure him. That black void made him dizzy. He dialed again.

"Fifth Precinct, Sgt. Klaus." Another calm voice. Rick expected everyone to be as anxious as he was even though he realized everyone else didn't know yet that they should be panicked.

"Sergeant, my name is Rick Sierra. I have a daughter who is six. She's missing." Rick kept his words to a minimum. Partly because he didn't want to waste time. Partly because he couldn't talk without sounding shaky.

"When did you discover her missing?"

"This morning. I think she may have tried to walk to school on her own."

"Roosevelt?"

"Yes. The principal says she's not there."

"O.K. Mr. Sierra, what's your daughter's name and what was she wearing?"

"Kathy, and I don't know. She wasn't dressed yet when I left to take my wife to work. She usually wears a light purple jacket that has a Minnie Mouse picture on the front. She has reddish brown hair and brown eyes. And she just lost a front tooth."

"Let me get the radio active on this quickly. Please hold." From the background noise on the telephone, Rick could hear the sergeant making a call on the radio to those in the area of Roosevelt Elementary to be on the lookout for Kathy.

Sgt. Klaus' voice came back over the phone, "Would your wife have her by any chance?"

"No, I just got off the phone with my wife, and she's walking home from the hospital to cover the route they usually take together in the afternoon."

"Good idea. If you locate your daughter, call us immediately. In the meantime, we'll comb the neighborhood between your home and school. And we'll send a patrolman over to get a picture and fill out a report. What did you say your address was?"

Rick gave him the address. His mind racing but with no particular direction. Just be safe. Just be safe. *Oh, God, please let her be safe.*

Julie saw the patrol car parked in front of the house as she rounded the corner. She felt caught in a nightmare. If only she could force herself awake.

As she entered, Rick introduced her to the patrolman who took a moment to nod in her direction as he finished scribbling on his clipboard. Rick's arm immediately went around Julie and they could read the dread in each other's eyes.

"I was just asking your husband if he knew of anyone who might want to snatch your daughter, Mrs. Sierra," the patrolman said. He was about Rick's age and probably had children of his own.

"You think she's been kidnaped?" A knife internally somewhere was cutting through Julie's insides at the thought of other stories of kidnaped children. *Dear, God, no. Please, no.*

"My Sgt. Peters is questioning Mrs. Burke. As I understand, she claims you called this morning and told her not to come to stay with Kathy because a friend was taking her for the day. Did you call her?"

"No. Could Mrs. Burke be confused? She's always seemed very reliable to us but she is getting up in years," said Julie.

"Well, we'll have to see what Sgt. Peters says when she's done interviewing her. Right now, I could use some pictures to help our search."

"Sure," Rick said and went to the closet where they kept the boxes and albums of photographs.

Julie sank down into the couch as if the breath were knocked out of her. Like a yellow flash, Julie saw the Mustang convertible in her head. Suddenly her mind's eye went to the driver and, as if a camera had zoomed in for a close up, the face of the driver loomed large before her. She jumped up with a wail.

"What is it, honey?" Rick was by her side in a moment.

"The yellow Mustang, Rick," Julie moaned. "The driver. I just realized. It was her mother. It was Kathy's mother."

Three

Kathy's Mother

The last time Julie had seen Kathy's mother, she was coming out of the general anesthetic the doctor had administered. Sebrena was a beautiful woman, Julie remembered, dark hair, prominent cheek bones. She could easily have been a model.

Sebrena's physical beauty had certainly attracted the attention of Dr. Erving. Attracted him and blinded him. He never should have attempted that abortion so late into the pregnancy. Julie had sensed that there was more between the good doctor and Sebrena than just a normal patient and doctor relationship but never had the opportunity to investigate further.

Julie remembered that terrible, yet wonderful, night Kathy had been born.

"Nurse!" Get in here immediately! I need your assistance!" Dr Erving barked.

Julie put down her coffee and rushed to the delivery room. What is going on, she wondered. There was no one in the labor room tonight and she would have been notified of an emergency.

Reaching the door, she paused for a moment to take in what was happening. The woman on the table was obviously in heavy labor, moaning and thrashing about. The doctor was trying to calm her down.

"Quickly," the doctor said. "We need to give her a general. This delivery's not going right."

"I'll call for the anesthesiologist," Julie replied.

"No! There isn't time. I'll take the responsibility and administer it myself. Get over here and help me."

Julie was panicked. This wasn't proper procedure. Her mind raced as her eyes took in more of the scene before her. Obviously the urgency of the situation was accelerating. She was afraid for the patient as well as the baby and knew that moments were precious when a delivery was going bad. In a moment she was by the doctor's side helping him strap the woman's arms down and placing the mask over her face.

"Monitor her blood pressure and respiration and keep me posted as I get the fetus out of here," Dr. Erving ordered.

"Fetus?" Julie thought. Then horror struck her as her gaze fell upon the saline solution and instruments on the table next to the doctor. This wasn't a delivery gone bad. This was an abortion!

"Doctor, I can't take part in this. I don't believe in abortion," Julie began to protest. Since the hospital had begun to allow abortions, some of the nurses had protested and won the right to decline assignment to assist in the procedure. Julie would have preferred it be banned entirely but at least this was a workable compromise.

"This is not the time for a political statement. We're here to save lives," the doctor said working furiously beneath the canopy. "Right now this woman's life depends on how quickly we can get this fetus out. Concentrate on what you're doing and not on your confounded religious rubbish. What are her numbers?"

Julie repeated the blood pressure and respiratory counts to him. They were precarious but not life threatening yet. Ironic, Julie thought, you tell me we're here to save lives while you sit there taking one.

"Finally," Dr. Erving said with relief as he took the bloody form of a baby and roughly laid it in the bin normally used for disposing of the afterbirth. Julie felt sick. She concentrated on the gauges before her, trying not to think of what was happening. At least a midterm saline abortion was not as horrendous to watch as a midterm dilation and evacuation or partial birth. This baby would be in one piece.

Dr. Erving took a moment to wipe his forehead before delivering the afterbirth. As he leaned forward again, Julie glanced at the little body in the bin. She blinked. Had she seen a movement? Yes, the arms were moving slightly. As she maneuvered to get a better look, Dr. Erving dropped the mass of afterbirth onto the baby. She left her patient for a moment to get a closer look. Yes, it did look like there was movement.

"What are you doing?" Dr. Erving asked angrily.

"That baby is alive," Julie said reaching for it.

"Impossible."

"It is," Julie said grabbing a clamp for the umbilical cord and an aspirator off the pediatric cart. Working quickly, she cleared the mucus from the baby's nose and mouth and clamped and cut the cord. A healthy cry emitted from the little girl who was beginning to squirm.

"Leave that fetus alone and attend to this patient!" the doctor ordered.

"I won't. Your patient is doing fine. This is a live baby. You can't just let it die. You said it yourself. We're here to save lives."

"If we lose this woman it will be your fault. I'll see you pay," growled the irate doctor.

"Your patient is fine, doctor," said Julie as she noticed the woman beginning to rouse from the light general the doctor had administered. "If this baby dies, I'll see you before the board," Julie threatened. She was shaking as she placed the precious bundle in the receiving unit. She had never challenged a doctor like that before. Rick. She needed Rick. He was on call for pediatrics. She reached the nearest phone and dialed the doctors' lounge.

"Rick, I need you in the delivery room. I have a newborn that needs your attention." Julie said quickly.

"On my way," came his calm and reassuring reply.

Rick was specializing in pediatrics and had only a year left to finish and then be on his own. He would know what to do to help save this beautiful little creature in front of her.

Julie looked over at the mother. She seemed to be doing fine. Still groggy and not aware that Dr. Erving was stitching up an area where he had needed to make a small incision for the delivery. The doctor was sweating profusely now. Julie couldn't remember Dr. Erving being listed as a doctor that performed abortions for the hospital. Something wasn't quite right. She was sure he hadn't even reserved the room. If this were his first, he had really messed it up. Hopefully, it would be his last.

Julie stood by the baby's side making sure she wasn't in any distress. Maybe there was a good reason for her being called in here tonight. Maybe God had meant for her to see all this. And, maybe this was His way of providing the child that Rick and Julie so desperately wanted. An idea began to form in Julie's head.

"Dr. Erving, my husband is on his way here to help with the baby. If you agree to sign a birth certificate and help us arrange an adoption, I won't bring my complaint to the board about your attempt to let the baby expire."

"The board will side with me," Dr. Erving said. "Many of them have been in similar situations. You're only a nurse. It would be your word against mine. You don't have enough credibility to do me any damage."

"That may be true, but I am a member of the Right to Life group and I'm sure if my information were placed in the right hands, you and your patient would suffer some very damaging publicity." He glanced suddenly at the woman on the table. Her face now uncovered, she was dozing from exhaustion and leftover anesthetic. Julie knew she'd hit a nerve.

"That would end your nursing career. No hospital would ever hire you again," he said not wanting to look back at her.

"I'm willing to take that chance," Julie said, feeling more sure with each moment that this had to be what God had intended. "I believe life is that important."

Rick entered and immediately began attending to his tiny patient. Julie began to fill him in on what had just taken place.

"She's sweet, isn't she?" Julie said, "And she can be ours. Dr. Erving doesn't want anyone to know what happened here and certainly the mother doesn't want a live baby. What do you say?"

"I don't know, Julie." Rick started to say something else but then realized the baby had stopped breathing. Quickly he reacted and began resuscitating. "I've got to get her to PICU. We'll talk later."

Julie managed to get Dr. Erving's signature on a birth certificate form before he left his patient in recovery. She knew that the birth certificate would be essential later if Rick said yes to her plan.

The mother's chart was made out by Dr. Erving to indicate a miscarriage and the pertinent medical history filled in. As she watched Dr. Erving with the woman, Julie began to realize that the doctor knew this patient very well, very well indeed.

"A close friend," he had replied to her question about his relationship to the patient.

"Was it your baby?" she had asked.

"No!" he said emphatically, looking defensive. Julie thought otherwise, but took him at his word.

As soon as her shift ended, Julie headed directly for PICU.

"We can't, Julie," Rick said when she joined him in his all night vigil with the baby. "How would we explain a baby all of a sudden? The records. The hospital has to record the birth."

"We can say it was a prearranged private adoption. The mother had the baby at home and Dr. Erving brought it here when it had difficulty breathing. I can get all the papers filled out. See," she said drawing a document from the folder she was carrying, "I already have the form for the birth certificate."

"You are something else," Rick said smiling at her then looking wistfully at the little pink and purple bundle in the incubator. Inside a battle raged over his desire to keep the child and the gnawing feeling that it wouldn't work. It just wasn't right. But, if they turned the baby over to social services they would lose her.

"What should we name her? I still haven't filled that in." Julie was being insistent and hoping that Rick's quietness was affirmation of what she wanted to do.

"She's a Kathy if ever I saw one," Rick replied putting his arm around Julie. It has to be right, Julie thought. Rick even knows her name. *Thank you, God.*

Before heading home, Julie looked in on a sleeping Sebrena, Kathy's birth mother. She shook her head. What would drive a woman to want to destroy a life within her? Her own child? She would never understand. Except. . .a sudden thought occurred to her. Maybe there was something genetically wrong. If there were, having Sebrena's medical history would be a plus. Julie managed to photo copy it quickly before anyone missed it and went home feeling satisfied that she had thought of everything.

A weary Rick arrived home early in the morning. He had stayed most of the night by Kathy's side. It was obvious there had been a tender bonding between the two through the night and Julie took the opportunity to suggest they move quickly to have legal documents drawn up for adoption. Rick hesitated only a moment when she asked him to call David, his friend from college who had gone on to become a lawyer.

David was delighted to draw up the papers and since they were fairly standard he had them finished by the afternoon. Julie had used a fictitious name for the biological mother. And with David's paperwork in hand went about finding a notary public to witness a fake signature.

"You're such a brave lady," the notary said trying to be inconspicuous about wiping a tear from her eye. "Do the people you are giving the baby to understand that you are dying?"

Julie's lip trembled a bit from nervousness but the notary thought she was becoming emotional. She nodded her head. Her hair was tied up under a scarf with a hat over the top as though she was covering the baldness produced by kemo therapy.

"Doesn't the lawyer usually handle all the signatures. Usually they have a notary in their office." The notary's question sounded innocent but Julie's pulse quickened. What if she was discovered?

"That was just an option," Julie replied. "I just didn't think I could face everyone in the lawyer's office. I thought it would be easier this way if I did it privately." She fumbled in her purse for a tissue. Her eyes were beginning to water out of fear.

Seeing that the woman before her was getting very anxious and afraid that this would turn into a flood of tears from them both, the notary hurriedly affixed her seal and signature under the scrawled backhand that Julie had used to sign the name Sharon Smith.

"Thank you for being so understanding," Julie said. "You have made this a lot easier for me. I know this is the best thing for me to do. I don't know how much longer I'll be able to function normally and now at least whatever happens in the end, I'll know my little girt is loved and cared for."

The last statement had finished off the notary. Julie left her pulling tissues from the box in her drawer. Outside the office, Julie inhaled deeply. She clutched the papers to her chest and gave a sigh of relief.

Later that day another notary in David's office witnessed the signatures of both Rick and Julie. Now Kathy was all theirs as soon as they could take her home from the hospital.

Julie hadn't known then how important some of her actions would be. Sebrena's medical history could have important clues to where Kathy was. Fishing through the file, in the spare room upstairs, she located the papers. Should she hope that it was Sebrena who took Kathy? How would she even know Kathy existed? How could she have found them? Answers would come later. Right now finding Kathy was the only important thing. Dear God, please let this be the key.

As Julie came down the stairs, she could hear Sgt. Peters telling Rick how upset Mrs. Burke had been. She had called Mrs. Burkes's son before she left so that the woman wouldn't be alone until she calmed down. He worked close by and had arrived quickly.

"I think I know who may have taken her," Julie said entering the room. "Kathy is adopted and her biological mother may have tracked her down. I've seen a yellow Mustang convertible following us the last couple of days and I thought I recognized the driver. Now I'm sure it was her."

"Mrs. Burke said she remembered a yellow car in your driveway this morning when she was walking her dog. She assumed it was your friend who was supposed to take Kathy for the day," Sgt Peters said.

"Do you know where she lives?" the other patrolman asked.

"We moved to keep this sort of thing from happening. I only know the address from the town where Kathy was born. I have no idea where she might be now, but I can make some phone calls to try to track her down," Julie replied.

"O.K. Meanwhile, our first priority is to get this picture of your daughter circulating in the neighborhood. Did you catch a license number on that car?" Sgt. Peters asked.

"No. I'm sorry, I didn't"

"And, of course, Mrs. Burke didn't pay any attention because she thought nothing was wrong. It would explain the phone call this morning though. Obviously this woman was setting everything up to come in and take your daughter.

The officers left. Rick turned to Julie, his face mirroring her fear. If it was Sebrena, when they did find Kathy? Would they be able to get her back?

As soon as the police car pulled away, Julie began dialing the number listed on the medical form as Sebrena's home phone number. She waited impatiently for the ring on the other end.

"The number you have dialed, 555-6739, has been changed to 555-9920." The computerized voice repeated the new number one more time as Julie scribbled it down and then offered to dial it for her. Julie disconnected and began dialing the new number. So Sebrena had moved too. But, at least she hadn't been forced to move out of town. . .

Julie remembered what the head nurse at the hospital where Kathy was born told her. She had listened, unbelieving. She was sure she had taken care of all the paperwork so no one would suspect what had happened that night a year ago in the delivery room. How could there be any suspicion that the baby in the nursery actually belonged to the woman who had miscarried?

"Julie, I don't know what to tell you," Miss Simpson said. " I feel awful that someone would start horrendous gossip like this. I just thought you should know."

Julie and Rick agonized over what to do. Finally, they decided that the only way to be sure the story would die would be for them to leave. They decided to relocate in the southern part of the state. Rick would still have his license to practice within the state and he could set up his private practice in one of the larger cities there.

But they had not fully considered the cost of setting up a practice. With Rick's student loan to be paid and Julies paycheck just covering living expenses, there was no extra money for furnishing an office let alone buying the insurance he would need. The cost of buying into a practice was still out of the realm of possibility too. It was then that Rick had taken the job as a representative for a pharmaceutical company. They were living on bare necessities in order to save enough to at least buy into a partnership.

Julie shook the memories from her head as she finished dialing the new number. A young voice answered.

"Sebrena Jones, please," Julie said, "I'd like to speak with Sebrena Jones."

"She ain't here," the child answered.

"Can you tell me when she'll be back?" Julie asked.

"She don't live here. I ain't seen my mother since I was little. Don't want to see her neither," came the reply. Suddenly there was a scuffle on the line.

"Hello. Who is this?" insisted a booming male voice.

"Mr. Jones?"

"Yeah, I'm Harry Jones. Look, whoever you are, I don't appreciate you callin' and askin' my kid a bunch of questions about my ex-wife. You leave us alone. We haven't seen her and don't know where she is and we'd like to leave it that way." Before Julie had a chance to protest, he hung up.

Tears welled in her eyes. What would she do now? Kathy, where are you my sweetheart?

Four

Sebrena's House

"Wow!" exclaimed Kathy as she looked at the curved mahogany staircase that led to the open balcony above the foyer. The shiny marble floor reflected the huge brass chandelier that hung from the ceiling so very far above Kathy's head. It was just like the picture in her Cinderella book. She looked at the steps to make sure there was no glass slipper left behind.

"Come on," Sebrena said. "We'll put your new things in your room."

"My room?" Kathy skewered her face into a question mark.

"Yes. I have a room ready for you. Your Mommy and Daddy said you could stay with me a few nights. I forgot to tell you. That's why we had to stop at the store on our way home from the zoo. We forgot to pack the things you need."

Kathy seemed to look right through her. Sebrena hadn't counted on a child's perception being so keen. It had been easy to lie to her other children. They hadn't seemed to care about where she was going or with whom.

"I hafta go home." Kathy insisted. "Barnaby. I don't have Barnaby."

"Who is Barnaby?" Sebrena was on the edge of impatience.

"Barnaby is Wilbur's's friend. They have to be together."

"Wilbur. Barnaby. Where do you get all this stuff?" Sebrena rolled her eyes.

"Wilbur is a Pound Puppy. I adopted him. Don't you know?" Kathy responded with a sigh. How could anyone not know about Pound Puppies? You didn't just buy a Pound Puppy. You had to adopt it and promise to love it and take care of it. She wasn't sure staying here was such a good idea any more. Home was becoming very appealing.

"But, wait until you see what's in your room," Sebrena said, gently herding her up the stairs with the shopping bags.

They entered a creamy white room trimmed with a pink rose budded border at the ceiling. Soft pink organza curtains were pulled back at the window with satin ribbon and fastened to the wall with nosegays of pink rosebuds. A huge armoire sat against one wall accompanied by a large floor mirror. Two units of bookshelves lined the other wall with a small collection of children's books on one shelf and a few token knick knacks here and there. A high ceiling made the room look even more enormous from Kathy's perspective.

Sebrena crossed the room to the canopy bed summoning up what she felt was her most enthusiastic voice and said, "Well, look here. All these special friends on your bed just waiting for you to love them." Under the lace edged canopy on top of the billowy cream quilt, dotted with rosebuds, were four large stuffed animals propped up against the pink lacy pillow sham. One of them was a lion. "And here's a friend for Wilbur, too."

Sebrena picked up the stuffed lion and offered it to Kathy. She shook her head vigorously from side to side and clutched Wilbur tightly to her chest. "That's a lion. That's not a good friend for Wilbur and, besides, he already has a good friend. I need Barnaby," she insisted.

This was going nowhere and Sebrena found herself gritting her teeth to keep from being short with Kathy. She had spent days attending to the all the details to make this a little girl's dream room. Kathy didn't appreciate it for a moment. Well, she'll grow to like it, Sebrena thought. She knelt next to Kathy and forced a smile. "How about you putting away all these new things we bought and then later we can call Mommy and ask her to bring Barnaby over?"

Kathy hesitated, but then shook her head in agreement, still a little unsure of this new person in her life but satisfied for the moment.

"I need to go downstairs and put dinner in the oven so it will be ready when Wynne gets home. You'll like Wynne, Kathy. He's a lot of fun. If you're tired, you can take a little nap and I'll come up and get you when dinner is ready."

Kathy was left standing all alone in the big room, clutching Wilbur tightly. She brushed a tear away as it splashed down her cheek. It had been a fun day at the zoo, and buying all these new things was exciting, but now she wanted to go home. Maybe if she called Mommy, she'd change her mind about letting me stay, Kathy thought. She turned a circle in the room and spied a telephone on the desk in the corner.

She had practiced her phone number enough times to know it well. She carefully pushed the numbered buttons.

"Hello?" came Julie's anxious voice over the phone.

"Mommy, it's me," Kathy said. "Mommy, I want to come home."

"Kathy," Julie almost shouted as Rick raced to her side. "Kathy, honey, where are you?"

"At 'Brena's. We had a nice day at the zoo, but I don't want to stay here. I don't have Barnaby, and I want to come home." Kathy's voice was shaky and on the verge of breaking down. Julie felt sick inside.

"Honey, do you know what street you're on?" Julie quizzed her carefully, trying not to let her emotions overwhelm her.

"It's the street with big trees. Don't you know where 'Brena lives?"

"No, honey. Why don't you tell me the phone number and I'll call Sebrena for directions. Look on the phone Honey, and give me the number you see written on it." Julie grabbed for the pencil next to the phone.

"O.K. It's 5. . .6. . ." Kathy didn't have a chance to finish. Sebrena had seen the light on the kitchen extension flashing and went racing upstairs to Kathy's room.

"I need to talk to your mother," Sebrena said, taking the phone from Kathy. Putting herself between Kathy and the phone, she quickly disconnected the call, but continued a conversation as though she were talking to Julie.

"Yes, Julie, that would be fine. See you in a few days." Sebrena replaced the handset on the phone. "Mommy said she and Daddy are going on a little trip for a few days and they would like you to stay with me. Now, let's get these things put away and you can help me get dinner."

Tired and confused, Kathy silently helped to put stuffed animals on the shelves and clothes in the closet. Mommy's voice had sounded funny. And, why did she ask where I was? Maybe she forgot, Kathy thought. Grown ups did act strangely sometimes. Still, she wished she was home.

Julie's head slumped over the table as she sobbed deeply, the phone still clutched in her hand.

"What is it?" Rick asked frantically. "What did she say?"

"I couldn't. . .get. . .the number," Julie sobbed. "Someone. . .hung up."

Rick took the phone gently from Julie's hand and knelt beside her to embrace her. "Calm down now, sweetheart. Tell me what she said. Maybe we'll find a clue." He fought to keep control of his own emotions.

"Sebrena has her. She's at Sebrena's house on a street with big trees. All I got was 5-6 of the phone number. It doesn't tell us anything. How are we going to find her?"

"Well, first of all," Rick began, his analytical mind sharpened from all the years of searching out clues to diagnose the case studies presented in his classes, "we know she's O.K. We know she's at Sebrena's house—not a motel or restaurant or apartment. The house has to be in the local area. Kathy doesn't know how to dial long distance. And, it's an exchange that begins with 5-6. I'd say you learned a lot." Rick hugged her again.

"But is it enough? I've got to try Dr. Erving. He may just hang up on me but I have to try. I've always wondered if Kathy were his child even though he denied it. He's got to have some kind of information we can use."

"You won't be able to get him now. Office hours are over."

"He may be doing rounds at the hospital. I'll try there."

Julie's look of disappointment a few moments later told Rick she'd been unsuccessful. Dr. Erving was on vacation for a few days and not scheduled to return until the day after tomorrow. They would have to spend another day waiting for the information they were hopeful he could give.

"I'm going to give Mrs. Burke a call and let her know we know where Kathy is. Maybe she'll begin to get over feeling responsible. Then I'm going to fix you a cup of tea and a sandwich," Rick said.

"No, I don't care for anything. Thanks anyway."

"I'm going to fix one for both of us and you're going to try to eat a little with me. Neither of us is going to be able to help Kathy if we don't keep our strength up."

While Rick disappeared into the kitchen, Julie slowly climbed the steps to Kathy's room. She found Barnaby in the middle of the floor looking as forlorn as she felt. Cuddling the precious animal in her arms she sat on the rug and let the tears come.

Dear Lord, she prayed, *I don't understand why You're doing this, or allowing this. Kathy is ours. I know You meant for her to be ours. Didn't You? Please keep her safe. Help me to find her. She needs me, Lord. I'm her mother not that other woman who wanted her dead, who thought of her as an inconvenience she had to get rid of. Please, Lord, help us. Help us to find our little girl and bring her back home.*

Julie never had a reason to doubt God's help before. But this time a little seed of misgiving began to eat at her. Was she being punished? She pushed the thought quickly from her mind. God wouldn't do that? Would He?

Sebrena tucked the covers under Kathy's chin and around Wilbur. Kathy had insisted upon giving each of the new animals names before she finally nodded off to sleep. Where in the world did kids come up with all these names, Sebrena wondered. Kathy had seemed to really enjoy the stuffed hippopotamus. Herman, she had named it and had toted it around with the rag tag dog she clutched constantly. Sebrena felt good as she kissed Kathy gently on the forehead and backed out of the room quietly. She had finally done it. Kathy belonged to her, and she was now back in her rightful place. What the Sierra's had done was wrong.

Wynne would be so excited, Sebrena thought as she headed for the family room to wait for him. It was too bad he had to miss dinner with them but maybe this would be better. The two of them could have some time together alone, and she could work up to breaking the news to him that he now had a daughter. Kathy looked like such a little angel asleep upstairs. Wynne was sure to fall in love with her instantly. She will be the only child I will be able to give him, her face darkened. Dr. Erving had certainly botched everything.

Wynne whistled down the highway, content and very pleased with himself. He wasn't going over the hill at the age of 40, he was reaching his pinnacle. And, with any luck, maybe that pinnacle would be in Washington in a few years.

The small fund raiser for some of his other party members had been quite successful. He was looking forward to his huge spaghetti dinner that was sure to bring out a throng of campaign contributors. It would be affordable for those in his district and would give him a chance to appear as "the man of the people."

By attending some of the functions for other party members running in various offices, he was beginning to line up some strong support. Then there were the "you scratch my back, I'll scratch yours" deals to be made. Like that black woman judge running for reelection in the 8th district. Letting her hand out her flyers at his dinner wouldn't hurt anything and, who knows, she might be able to help me sometime. She looked like she was capable of going places in politics. He had been duly impressed. Had a good name too. Something French-sounding. Oh, yeah, Belmonte.

Arriving home, Wynne was happy to see Sebrena's Mustang in the garage. No night out with the girls tonight. He wished he'd been able to squeeze a few moments free to get her a dozen roses. A little token for the memorable night they'd had. Well, maybe they could make tonight memorable too and tomorrow he'd get her two dozen.

The word memorable stuck in his mind as Wynne sat frozen in his chair, wine glass in hand, while Sebrena finished relating her exciting news. She was so proud of herself and so full of anticipation. He knew she was expecting him to be thrilled and overjoyed with her accomplishment, but his mind was bouncing a million thoughts off the walls of his head all at once and most of them were not good. My God, what had she done? Kidnaping at the very least? But was it really kidnaping when the child had been hers to begin with? What was this going to do his career when the press got hold of it? Was there any way to stop that from happening? A daughter? I have a daughter?

"Why did you wait until now to tell me I have a daughter?" Wynne asked sharply, not quite sure what he was feeling at the moment.

"Darling, it was only recently I could confirm that our daughter was alive. Up until then, it was all just gossip. Who would have imagined that a nurse and a doctor would steal a baby and cover it up by claiming a miscarriage."

"But why didn't you tell me you were pregnant then before I left for Europe?"

"I wasn't sure that I was and I wasn't certain that you were coming back. Then, when they told me I had miscarried, I just didn't want to talk about it. I know this is a lot to understand all at once, Honey, but come and see how beautiful she is." Sebrena set his wine glass on the table and tugged gently on his hand to ease him out of the chair and lead him up the stairs to Kathy's room.

Wynne looked down at the sleeping form. Yes, he thought, she is pretty. But he could also see RESPONSIBILITY flashing in neon red. Their freedom would be cut drastically with the burden of a child to care for. This was not in his life plan at this time. Still, Sebrena, seemed so excited. She was holding him around the waist and pressing her warm soft body gently against his. The familiar smell of her touched his senses. He loved her so much. How could he deny her this?

Fingertip to her lips, Sebrena nudged Wynne from Kathy's room. Neither of them said anything until they reached their bedroom and closed the door. Where should he begin? What should he say?

"Darling, she is very pretty. Someday I'll bet she'll be as beautiful as her mother. But, you know we'll have to resolve this matter somehow legally. There must be records and a birth certificate naming the Sierras as mother and father. Perhaps we can settle it privately. I'm sure the Sierras don't want to be dragged through court after what they've done." Wynne sure hoped they wouldn't. If it wasn't too late already, maybe he could save himself from the dreaded media monster. "And we need to talk seriously about whether we have room for a child in our lives right now."

"I knew you'd understand," Sebrena said kissing his slightly stubbled chin, ignoring his last remark. She laid her head on his firm chest and fumbled with his shirt buttons until her fingers were inside delicately playing with the hair of his chest. She was pleased with herself and especially pleased with the idea that Wynne was ready to fight for her.

Sebrena would be the only one sleeping well that night as the autumn wind restlessly stirred the dry leaves from the big trees. Across town, leaves scraped against the screen door as Rick closed the telephone directory and tried to coax Julie to rest.

Five

Search

"I found two areas whose phone exchange begins with 5-6," Rick said closing the phone directory. "I'm going to cruise through those areas this morning and see if I can find a street with big trees. Maybe I'll be able to spot Kathy." Rick took another sip of his coffee and decided that was enough. His stomach was churning badly. It was as dismal outside as it felt inside. A cold steady rain was making everything gray, diminishing the colors of autumn and knocking down many of the leaves that had adorned the trees with bright orange, red and yellow. Gray clouds blocked the sun and made the sky foreboding.

"Shouldn't we call Sgt. Billings and tell him that Kathy called?" Julie asked again. Sgt. Billings, a rather stern and stout man who looked like he spent most of his time behind a desk, had stopped in last evening to update them on the search for Kathy and question them further. He had made them uncomfortable with his interrogation, as though he suspected them of foul play in Kathy's disappearance. Julie realized they probably looked a little guilty and answered haltingly at times when questioned about Kathy's mother. As much as Julie believed in her heart that God had wanted them to have Kathy, she still could feel a tinge of doubt about the way they had made Kathy theirs.

"Exactly how old was Kathy when you adopted her?" Sgt. Billings had asked Julie, his eyes penetrating hers as though he could read the answers there.

"She was only a few days old." Julie bit her trembling lip.

"Did the mother know who was adopting her baby? Did she know your names?"

"Not to my knowledge. The adoption was handled through our lawyer." Julie felt her face blush. She wasn't lying, exactly. Sebrena thought Kathy was dead. She wouldn't have known we adopted her.

Sgt. Billings continued to look at her as though he expected her to say something else. She diverted her gaze to Rick who had his head in hands staring at the floor in front of him. Billings sighed deeply and closed his notebook. He rose and advised them to try to get some sleep. He would call as soon as there was any news. As much as he had made Julie squirm, she still felt a sense of comfort in his aura of authority.

"No," Rick replied, "I think it would be better if we can handle this on our own now that we know for sure who we are dealing with. You stay by the phone in case Kathy should call again. I'll be back around noon." Rick hugged her trying to transfer as much love and strength as he could muster. Julie hadn't slept more than an hour. Neither had he, for that matter, but she looked so desperate, so fearful. His heart ached. He had to find Kathy this morning. *Please, God, show me where she is*, he prayed silently on his way out.

Julie thought about taking a shower, then decided against it. She wouldn't be able to hear the phone ring in the shower. She did the best she could to refresh herself at the bathroom sink even adding a little touch of makeup. She looked ghastly, dark circles under eyes swollen from crying. Somewhere she had to gather the energy to face this day. Somewhere, she knew, she had to find hope to keep her going.

The ringing phone startled her. She raced to answer it, anxiety sending a prickly sensation through her arms and spine.

"Mrs. Sierra, this is Sgt. Billings. I need your permission to release Kathy's picture and story to the news media. If we get them involved, we may be able to find her sooner." Billings cleared his throat while he waited for an answer.

"Could we wait just a little longer?" Julie asked. "I have a couple of phone calls to make that may help us find her. I'd hate to have the publicity scare Kathy's mother into something drastic." She was torn between wanting to use the media and yet worried that, if they were drawn in, they might investigate too far and she would loose Kathy anyway.

"Are you sure it was Kathy's mother who took her?" Billings asked. "She's been gone 24 hours now. I would think you might have had some contact with her."

"I'm sure that's who's been following us." Julie knew her voice was cracking. She tried to clear her throat. She couldn't betray Rick but she wanted desperately to tell the sergeant that Kathy had called. There was the nagging fear for Kathy's life. She had no way of knowing what Sebrena wanted with her child. If she were emotionally unstable, Kathy might be in danger. Julie had read about the trauma caused by the emotional stress of an abortion being repressed for years and then exploding.

"Of course, it's up to you and your husband, Mrs. Sierra," Sgt. Billings said with an exaggerated sigh and a long pause that made Julie hold her breath. "Are you sure you've told me everything? Is there something else I should know?"

"Hopefully, we will all know more in a little while, Sgt. Billings. We've told you all we know for now." Was she convincing enough? He sounded so suspicious. Had he found out something about the adoption? "I'll talk to Rick about the pictures and get back to you soon. Thank you." Julie was relieved that he didn't press farther. She had barely removed her hand from the phone when it rang again.

"Hello," Julie said, praying to hear Kathy's voice."Mrs. Sierra?" said a deep masculine voice.

"Yes, who is this?"

"I'm calling to let you know Kathy is safe. We're taking good care of her and. . ."

"Who are you? What do you want with my daughter?" Julie screamed into the phone.

"You will know who I am soon enough. For now, it's enough to know I am Sebrena's husband. As soon as we can get some legal advice, we will be contacting you again. I just wanted to extend the courtesy of letting you know Kathy was not in any danger."

The line clicked before Julie had a chance to ask any more questions. Not in any danger. I hope not. Legal advice? *Dear Lord, they're going to try to take*

Kathy away from us! Please send Rick home soon.

Rick turned the corner of another tree lined street. Every street on this side of town must be tree lined, he thought. Large homes graced Walnut Lane. Most of them were tudors. All of them with neatly manicured yards. There didn't seem to be an abundance of children playing in those yards but then, Rick thought, it is Saturday morning and cartoons were still running. He thought of Kathy tuned in to the weekend menu of cartoons. Was that what she was doing now? This was probably futile. He should just turn around and go back to be with Julie.

Suddenly he spotted a little girl on a scooter, pushing and gliding down the sidewalk. Kathy! It was Kathy! Quickly he pulled over and stopped. He jumped out of the car, not bothering to close the door. The pinging of the key alarm followed him as he rushed across the street. He caught the little girl by the shoulders and spun her around. She began screaming. One look at her freckled face and Rick realized his mistake.

"I'm sorry, honey, I thought you were someone else." The apology did no good. She continued screaming. Rick decided he'd better leave—fast. He didn't need to be dragged to the closest precinct for child molesting. Jumping back into his car, he spun away from the curb not noticing the curved drive leading to a brick colonial with a yellow Mustang parked by the front door.

Sebrena heard the screams of a little girl outside. She ran to the window to be sure it wasn't Kathy. Squealing tires added to the noise of the screams. As she looked out she could see a neighbor already comforting the little girl who lived just a few doors away. She probably just ran into a bee, Sebrena thought. They were vicious this time of year.

Kathy was still in her bed when Sebrena checked. She wondered how long she would sleep. She must have kept her up too late waiting for Wynne. Wynne had been so wonderful. She knew she could count on him. He would find a way to get Kathy back for her—legally. He had to. She didn't like losing.

She would prove that she could be a good mother. Harry would see that he had been wrong about her. Not that Harry mattered anymore. The pious fool could keep the kids he was raising to become just like him. She pictured the three of them, single file, huge Bibles tucked under their arms, marching into the little fundamental church he insisted on attending every Sunday morning and evening. When they were married, he had not only expected her to be there twice every Sunday but on every Wednesday as well whether she wanted to go or not. Well, religion was nice in moderation. It had it's time and place in life. But Harry carried it to the extreme and had even used it against her in court.

So, she had made a few mistakes. Nothing she should be condemned for. The biggest mistake was marrying Harry. Who could blame her for wanting a more exciting relationship? Harry even had to pray before they made love. He certainly took all the spontaneity out of it. Every time a problem came up, Harry had a scripture verse to throw at her. She had to admit to a deep sense of satisfaction when she told Harry of her affairs with Dr. Erving and Wynne.

Harry stumbled through his scripture verse, red faced, and couldn't finish because he was stuttering so badly.

His religious fanaticism had helped her in one cause—the divorce. Harry was absolved of any guilt because of her adultery and the abortion. Therefore he didn't fight the divorce, but he did fight for the kids. He issued an ultimatum. Either she relinquish her rights to the children or he would go to Wynne and make a scene about the abortion. She couldn't let Wynne find out about Dr. Erving or the pregnancy. Actually, she had come out ahead since Wynne hadn't wanted a ready-made family. And Wynne was worth the sacrifice.

Harry had his little carbon copies of himself, but Kathy was hers. Harry couldn't take that away from her, and she certainly wouldn't give him the chance to turn this child into a Bible thumping idiot. As far as Harry knew this child was dead.

Kathy turned over and stretched. She blinked a few times as though trying to decide where she was.

"Good morning, angel," Sebrena said sweetly. Kathy looked at her with a sudden realization of where she was. Her eyes teared up again and she buried her head in Wilbur.

"I want to go home," Kathy whimpered.

"Now, you know that Mommy and Daddy are away. You can't go home today, Kathy, so let's just make the best of it," Sebrena was exercising patience as best she could. Once she understands that I'm her real mother, Sebrena reasoned, she'll be very happy to stay. "C'mon Kathy, let's go down and have some breakfast."

Kathy slowly raised her head and began pulling her feet out of the covers. She took Sebrena's outstretched hand and followed her down the stairs to the kitchen.

"What would you like? How about some eggs and bacon or some pancakes?" Sebrena was anxious to begin being the perfect mother, starting with making a good breakfast.

"Cereal," said Kathy.

"Cereal isn't a real breakfast."

"I like cereal. It's what I have every morning."

"O.K.," said Sebrena giving into the stubborn look on Kathy's face. "What kind of cereal would you like?"

"Cheerios."

"Cheerios? I don't have any Cheerios." Sebrena was becoming exasperated. "I have some raisin bran and oatmeal. Which would you like?"

"I don't like those kind," Kathy replied with a shake of her head that almost twisted the rest of her off the chair.

"That's all I have," said Sebrena beginning to lose control. "Take it or leave it."

"I'll have the yucky raisin bran," Kathy conceded. "Can I watch cartoons after I eat?"

"Yes," Sebrena said. That was better than having Kathy outdoors and risk the chance of her being seen by neighbors or, worse, by the police who were probably out looking by now. She paused, cereal bowl midair. What if they alerted the media? Kathy would see herself on TV. Maybe she should let the Sierras know the score. They certainly wouldn't want the attention the media would give them. She set the bowl down. No, she reasoned, they probably hadn't told the news people yet. It would have been front page headlines this morning, and she would have seen it.

Rick picked up the morning paper as he entered the house. Julie came running the minute she heard the door open.

"Any luck?" She could tell by his look what his answer would be.

"No. I saw a little girl I thought was Kathy. Lucky I didn't get arrested. The girl started screaming when I grabbed her shoulder. She wouldn't stop. I don't think I'd better drive through that neighborhood again."

Any other time, Julie would have teased him. She was too desperate to see any humor in the situation.

"How are things here?" he asked seeing the intensity in Julie's eyes.

"I got an awful phone call."

"Kathy?"

"No. Sebrena's husband."

"What did he want? Surely he's not asking for a ransom?"

"A ransom would probably be easier. He's looking into legal counsel to try to get Kathy back. He wouldn't tell me his name or anything else. Just that we would hear from him soon and that Kathy was safe and sound. He felt some kind of obligation to tell us that. Rick I'm so scared."

Rick sat down on the couch as though someone had knocked the wind out of him. Julie joined him. They held hands and sat in silence for a few moments, tears filling their eyes.

"Well, what do we do next?" Rick asked.

"I don't know. I want Kathy back. I'm not giving up without a fight. Let's keep on trying to find them. Maybe if we can snatch her back we can move again."

"That's not going to work. They found us once. They'd find us again. Besides, what would we be doing to Kathy?"

"But we have all the papers that say Kathy is ours. They can't possibly have much to go on for a court battle. And Kathy needs to be with us. We're her family—the only one she knows."

"You're right, we have papers. The question is will they hold up in court? Is there any way we can get hold of Dr. Erving? That seems to be our best chance to track Sebrena down. Maybe there's some way we can work things out."

"I'll try some other people I used to work with. Someone might be able to help me locate him." Julie went to the hall phone and began looking up numbers in her old address book.

Rick bent over and put his head in his hands. *Lord, I've prayed so much these last twenty-four hours that I'm not sure what to pray anymore. Julie and*

I may have been wrong in the way we adopted Kathy, but Kathy is so precious to us. Please, Father, watch over her. Guide us to her and show us what your will is for all of us. We only want what is best for Kathy and I know You do too. Help us to accept whatever You decide. In Your precious Son's name. Amen."

Julie came in just as Rick sat up again. "I've got it," she announced triumphantly. "I've got Dr. Erving's home phone number. There's no answer right now, but I'll keep trying."

Julie tried until midnight, finally giving up with the presumption that the doctor still had not returned from his vacation. She slipped into bed next to Rick. *Why, Lord, why is this happening? I was so sure it was Your will for us to have Kathy. Everything worked out right. How could I have been wrong? Right or wrong, please watch over our little girl.* Closing her eyes, she drifted off into another night of fitful sleep.

At the fifth precinct station, a copy of a missing person's file, was exchanged for a handful of $20 bills. "I don't know if it will pan out to be anything, but there is an unusual circumstance with the child being adopted and the birth mother showing up." The man in uniform tucked the currency into his pocket and pulled a paper cup full of hot coffee from the vending machine.

"Thanks," said the man standing next to him in khakis and a rumpled knit shirt. His blonde hair was short but looked like it hadn't seen a comb that day. Maybe that was because he kept running his hand through it. "Your leads usually give me some kind of a story. You seem to have a reporter's sixth sense. Maybe you missed your calling." He playfully thumped the other's badge. He popped some change into the coffee machine, hesitating over the hot chocolate button before hitting the one for black coffee. Black coffee was a man's drink. Hot chocolate was for kids.

"Just make sure you forget where you got that and make sure it disappears quick."

"Hey, no sweat. Have I ever implicated you before? And, if this doesn't turn out to be anything news worthy, maybe I can use it for my next novel."

"Yeah, right." The cop looked around the doorway of the alcove where the vending machines spewed out coffee and stale sandwiches and assortments of junk food. He walked quickly down the hall and up the stairs.

A moment later, Michael Boston tucked the papers under the jacket he was carrying and exited the alcove, moving down the hall in the opposite direction. Adrenaline pumping, he skipped down the stairs, out the front door and into the night.

Six

Kathy's Return

"Erving residence," the antiseptic voice said. Dr. Erving must have married his receptionist, Julie thought. *I could never forget that voice. How could someone who seemed devoid of emotion work in an obstetrician's office?*

Julie raised her fist triumphantly in the air as a signal to Rick that she's finally gotten through. They had skipped morning worship service. Too many people would ask where Kathy was and neither of them wanted to face any explanations this morning. Julie kept calling the doctor's phone number every half hour. Her persistence had finally paid off.

"Is Dr. Erving in?" Julie asked.

"May I ask who's calling?"

"This is Western Union. I have a telegram for Dr. Erving." Julie was afraid that if she gave her name, he would refuse to talk with her. She waited.

"Hello, this is Dr. Erving."

"Dr. Erving, this is Julie Sierra. Do you remember me?" There was a long pause. Julie held her breath, hoping that he wouldn't hang up on her.

"Oh, yes, how could I forget you," he answered with an emphasized note of sarcasm to his voice. "Just what do you want?"

"Dr. Erving, Sebrena has somehow discovered that her daughter is alive. She found us and we suspect that she's abducted Kathy."

"Well, isn't that just too bad. Maybe this is your payback for interfering in other people's lives."

"Doctor, I don't have time to argue. She has obviously remarried and moved. Do you have any idea what her new name is or where she lives now?"

"Why would I? I haven't seen her in years. And, why should I help you anyway?"

Julies' heart beat faster as anger began to well up inside. "We have the police involved in the search. I haven't told them all the background on Kathy's entrance into this world and your part in it, but if you aren't going to help me out directly, then I'll have to give them your name and explain your involvement. Who knows what they might end up investigating."

"I've always remembered you as arrogant and self righteous. Still the blackmailer, too. You haven't changed. I'll give you what you want but you had better keep me out of this. I don't want anything more to do with that woman or with you."

Julie wrote furiously with Rick leaning over her shoulder trying to decipher what she was recording. "You want to tell me what this chicken scratch means," Rick said moving the paper up and down in front of him. "Your handwriting could get you half way to a doctor's degree."

"Sebrena, apparently, was two-timing our good doctor. Shortly after Kathy's birth, he accidently ran into her at a restaurant and she introduced her date. He's pretty sure the man was the one she married after her divorce. Dr. Erving thinks the man's name was Wander or Werner or something that sounds like that. He remembers he was in the advertising business and had his own company . Sebrena rubbed it in about how successful he was. What do you think? Can we find them?"

Rick was already looking for the yellow page directory. Let's see what kind of ad agencies we have listed in town."

They didn't have far to look before they found the "Anderson and Warner Ad Agency" listing.

"Warner is close enough. Write it down, Jul, while I look at the rest of them." There was nothing else listed with a name that came close to what they were searching for. There were a few agencies that were not named after the partners. They listed those just in case Warner didn't pan out.

"Now," Rick said, "let's look in the residential listings and see if there's a Warner with a 5-6 exchange."

"Bingo!" Julie exclaimed. "Warner, Wynne, on Walnut Lane. Sounds kind of hokey."

"Walnut Lane? That's the street I was on when I saw the little girl I thought was Kathy. I passed right by there! Should we call or just go over and try to get Kathy?"

"If we call, Sebrena's liable to run with her. I think we need to pay a visit." Julie grabbed her purse and the paper with the address. Rick pulled out his keys and opened the door for Julie as they headed for the car. A startled figure greeted them with a hand still raised to knock on the door.

"Morning."

"Good morning," Rick responded. "I'm sorry but whatever this is about will have to wait. We are on our way out. Can we catch you another time?" Rick assumed it was either a salesman or a Jehovah Witness, although either seemed unlikely on a Sunday morning.

"Sure. Let me give you my card," he said pulling a business card from his pocket. "I had hoped we might be able to talk for a few moments about your daughter."

Julie's head began to throb. She strained to look at the name on the card Rick held. "News Herald" it read. The reporter's name was in the corner in smaller letters, Michael Boston.

"What do you know about our daughter?" Rick demanded.

"Just that she's been reported missing. I thought I might be able to help by running a story and a picture."

"Well, we appreciate your offer, Mr. Boston, but our daughter is no longer missing. It was just a big misunderstanding. I'm sorry if you've wasted your time, but thanks again."

"No problem. Glad to know this one had a happy ending. Nice to have good news to report for a change."

Rick tensed. "We'd prefer you not write about this. We don't want to cause our daughter or anyone else involved any embarrassment over this mix up. You understand, don't you?"

"Sure thing, Mr. Sierra. Guess I'll have to hit the pavement for another story. Nice talkin' to you."

Rick and Julie closed the door and stared at each other for a moment. They each held their breath waiting to hear a car start and pull away. When the familiar sound assured them he was gone, they rushed out the door to their car. They were both tense as they turned onto the east-west freeway.

"I hope we convinced him to keep this out of the paper." Julie said.

"I'm sure he'll find a much more exciting story by this afternoon and forget all about us," Rick said trying to reassure himself as well.

"Are you sure you drove out of Walnut Lane before anyone saw you this morning?" Julie said, a slight smile on her face.

"Why?" Rick turned to see the glint in her eye. "Are you afraid of being seen with a suspected child molester?"

"You got it. You could turn out to be that exciting afternoon story." She reached over and patted his knee. The teasing eased the tension until they turned onto Walnut Lane. Both Julie and Rick stiffened with the anticipation of facing Sebrena again.

It had not been a good morning for Sebrena. She had let Kathy talk her into attending a church service. Feelings of deja vu assaulted her throughout the service as she shrugged off the memories of Harry.

I needed to get Kathy and Wynne separated for a while, Sebrena thought, drumming her fingers on the pew in front of her as she impatiently waited for the minister's prayer to end. Wynne and Kathy shared some kind of natural animosity toward each other. Kathy seemed to know just how to prod Wynne and irritate him. He didn't say anything but she could tell that Kathy was getting on his nerves. That was the reason she finally gave into Kathy's request to attend church services.

"We always go as a family," Kathy had said as she dressed. "Isn't Wynne coming too?"

"No, he has work to do this morning," Sebrena said giving Wynne an excuse. Kathy didn't press. Either she was glad he wasn't coming or it wasn't important to her. Joseph and Rachael would have pressed. But, then, Harry had indoctrinated his children with the absolute fear of God. Maybe the Sierras hadn't been so obnoxious about their religion.

At least taking Kathy to church would prove she had nothing against religion, or God for that matter, but she would certainly choose carefully which church they would attend. No "holy rollers" for her.

As the last hymn was begun, Sebrena gently tugged on Kathy's arm. "We have to leave, darling," Sebrena whispered. She didn't want to be stopped on the way out. Kathy just might say something she wouldn't be able to explain. Quietly the two slipped out into the aisle and through the back door. Kathy seemed content, almost happy, as she plopped into the front seat and buckled her seat belt.

"That was a nice service," Kathy said as Sebrena started the car. "But our church is a lot more friendly. And we go to Sunday School. I have a nice teacher. She. . ."

Kathy rambled on while Sebrena made a mental note to check the church out a little more. It might be a good possibility for them when Kathy was finally theirs. After all, it couldn't hurt Wynne's political career to have a connection to a church as long as it wasn't radical. And, church going would be a good image in her role as mother. She remembered what Wynne had said last night when he returned from the lawyer's office.

"Ed says we have a good case, but he will have to meet with you and get all the information he can to put together a good presentation. There may be the possibility of pressing criminal charges against the Sierras. A lot will depend on that doctor and the staff at the hospital having good memories."

Sebrena thought about Charles Erving. Poor Charles. He wasn't terribly exciting but he had been in love with her. She was sure of that. She regretted using him the way she did but she had no alternative. There was no way she could afford an abortion on her own, and she knew that once Wynne returned from setting up a European office in Paris, he would know she had let Harry into her bed again.

Wynne had promised to help her through her divorce when he returned. She had a small window of time to work with but the doctor had been obviously interested in her for a long time so it didn't take much to get him to make love to her, win his sympathy, and his support for the abortion. Obviously she should have worked a little faster and not let the pregnancy get so far along. But, in the end, she still got what she wanted. Wynne, her divorce, and now maybe even the child she thought she could never have. Would Charles give them the deposition she needed? Not without a struggle. How was she going to keep him from revealing that the "miscarriage" was really a planned abortion?

"Daddy!" Kathy yelled startling Sebrena as they pulled into the drive. "That's Daddy's car!".

Sebrena's first impulse was to put the car in reverse and gun it out of the driveway. But, Kathy was so excited, she was already opening the car door and jumping out. Sebrena tripped going up the stairs trying to keep up with her. Kathy was in Julie's arms before Sebrena had a chance to say a word.

"So you found us," Sebrena said flatly looking at Wynne for a sign that everything was all right. Wynne stared at Sebrena. She couldn't read his expression but she could tell by the tone of his voice that he was determined to command the situation. What had been going on? What had the Sierras told him?

"Kathy, why don't you say good-bye to Sebrena and wait outside for us for a moment," Julie said.

"Kathy's not leaving," Sebrena began to say, but Wynne cut her off.

"Yes, she is," he said sternly. The Sierras are home from their trip now. Kathy can come and stay another time." He looked down at Kathy and forced a smile across his face.

Sebrena hugged Kathy and patted her auburn curls. "I'll see you again. . . soon," she said.

"Wilbur is in the car waiting for you with the rest of your things," Julie said holding the door open for Kathy. When the door closed, the air became thick with hostility. Julie broke the silence.

"How did you find out about Kathy?" she asked Sebrena.

"An anonymous phone call a few years ago. I didn't think anything of it until I ran into Charles, Dr. Erving," Sebrena quickly corrected. "He told me Kathy was alive and had been adopted." She failed to mention that the reason Dr. Erving had told her was that he was so angry when she rejected him, he had blurted out the whole truth hoping to hurt her as much as she had hurt him.

"Coincidence put us in the same town, and I saw you one day at the hospital when I went for some tests. There was something about you that was just very familiar. I got your name, connected you with the hospital where Kathy was born and then started following you home. I'll let you have Kathy for now, but we will see each other in court so that I can prove my rights as her mother."

Sebrena smiled resolutely as she moved closer to Wynne and put an arm around him. He was an impressive opponent, and she wanted to emphasize the importance of him being on her side. She was sure, with Wynne's political influence and money, the Sierra's didn't stand a chance.

"Of course," Wynne said putting his arm around Sebrena, "We could settle this out of court and make it easier on everyone. After all, there will probably be some criminal charges brought up also. I'm sure the two of you don't want to face that."

"Criminal charges! If anyone should be charged with a crime it should be you Sebrena. Not only for kidnaping but for attempted murder!" Julie was red with anger. All the fear and frustration of not knowing where Kathy was all this time was exploding.

"I beg your pardon," Sebrena said sarcastically. "It was you who did the original kidnaping and I don't recall anyone ever having a miscarriage being convicted of attempted murder."

"Is that what you're calling it? The records may show that you had a miscarriage but we both know that it was your lover who botched the abortion that led to Kathy's being born alive. You wanted her dead. You're not fit. . ."

"Julie, we'd better leave. Now." Rick firmly took her arm The argument was getting louder, and he didn't want any of this to reach Kathy's ears.

Julie felt like she was suffocating. There was nothing more she could do but let Rick lead her out. As they reached the door, Rick turned and calmly said, "Kathy is our daughter, and we are the only family she knows. We won't give her up without a fight."

"You're forgetting one important thing," Sebrena almost shouted, "I'm her mother. Her only mother. I gave birth to her. She's rightfully mine."

Sebrena and Wynne watched as the Sierras drove off with Kathy. Sebrena stood for a moment, back stiff , bathed in righteous indignation. Then she suddenly began to realize what Wynne had heard. She closed the door as Wynne turned away, shoulders slightly slumped, looking weary. In his mind the questions were running. Were the Sierras right? Was it an abortion? How far was he willing to go? How much was he willing to risk for this beautiful woman he had fallen in love with?

He looked pleadingly at Sebrena. "Is there anything more you need to tell me about this?"

"They're lying. The records show that it was a miscarriage. They have Kathy's birth mixed up with someone else." Charles had better back her up. She'd take him to court for malpractice and anything else she could if he didn't.

Wynne wanted to believe her. This magnificent woman who had brought so much joy into his life. But, if she had truly tried to abort Kathy when there was no good reason for it, how was he going to forgive her? Many believed he stood behind the pro choice line but in reality he avoided taking a strong stand either way. Not a good political move, but he couldn't fathom a woman taking a life within her and destroying it just because it was inconvenient or not financially feasible, not when so many others wanted to adopt children. Oh, how he wanted to believe her.

As the Sierras pulled away from the Warner's home, Mike Boston let out a long low whistle. Obviously, the daughter had been here all along and, if what he had learned so far was true, that would make Wynne Warner's wife the biological mother who snatched her. A misunderstanding, as Sierra had put it, was an understatement.

Furiously he began to make notes to capture the ideas and questions running through his head. Sebrena Warner's maiden name? Previously married? Other children? Reasons for giving up daughter? Warner's love child? Custody battle? Check court for papers filed. How would this affect Warner's political aspirations? Get responses from party chairman.

He toyed with the idea of going up to the door and firing some questions at the Warners, but decided it would be best to do some investigative work first. "Yes, sir, my man in blue never lets me down," he said as he smiled at himself in the mirror.

Seven

Mother? Mother?

Julie awoke feeling heavy—too heavy to lift herself out of bed. It was hard to tell if she had kept Rick awake or he had been the one to keep her awake most of the night tossing back and forth. Each time she would begin to doze, she would dream. But they weren't dreams. They were nightmares. And Sebrena haunted every one of them.

After arriving home, Rick and Julie had given Kathy a stern lecture about going off with anyone without first checking with them. The poor child was confused about what she might have done wrong. Sebrena had certainly manipulated and plied Kathy with her lies.

Julie restrained herself from calling Sebrena a liar in front of Kathy. She tried to absolve Kathy's feeling of guilt by blaming Sebrena for getting things confused. She didn't want to frighten Kathy of Sebrena if things went totally sour and Kathy were to end up with the Warners. She numbed at the thought. But, she couldn't have Kathy living in fear. She and Rick would have to be careful.

As Julie lay in bed trying to will her body to lift itself, she kept rerunning the previous day's conversation with Sebrena. "Coincidence," Sebrena had said. Coincidence had put them in the same town. Julie didn't believe in coincidences. If she truly believed in God directing her path, she would have to believe that He had caused their paths to cross. But why?

Confusion clouded Julie's thoughts. She had been so grateful that Rick had taken command and was thinking logically. As soon as he had called the police station, explaining that Kathy had been returned and there would be no charges filed, he had called David. David would be involved legally too, even though he had ben an innocent accomplice. Would he help them? Could he help them? David told Rick he would call back.

Julie finally swung her legs over the side of the bed, her toes just brushing the carpet. She felt a little dizzy as her head came up off the pillow to follow the rest of her body into a somewhat vertical position. She had to get up and get Kathy off to school. She had already decided she was not going into the hospital today. She would take her accumulated sick days and vacation until this was over. She was not going to leave Kathy alone again.

"But how cum you're not going to work? Don't you feel good? Can I stay home and take care of you? Do you want me to make breakfast? I can make toast for me and Daddy." Kathy was certainly her old self this morning, Julie thought.

"Just sit still, Kathy," Julie said as she plodded through the motions of filling a cereal bowl with Cheerios and milk. "I'm just a little tired and I think I need to take a little vacation so I can spend some more time with you."

"Vacation? Where are we going? Disney World? I would love to go to Disney World? Mickey Mouse lives there! When can we go? Is Daddy coming too?" Quiet came only after she dove into her little bowl of "o"s.

Rick finally left for work, Kathy riding with him as far as school. Julie sank into a kitchen chair with her second cup of coffee and reached for her Bible. I don't even know what to read, she decided, closing the well worn book and pushing it away. I should be praying. How can I pray? I don't know what to pray for. She stared into her coffee cup.

Why would you do this Lord? Why would you give Kathy to us only to take her away? I don't see how we can ever expect to keep her now. We can't fight the Warners' political influence or the power their money can buy. The tears began to slide down her cheeks. This is what she had wanted to avoid facing. The possibility of losing their most precious possession.

Julie thought back to her outburst in the Warners' living room. She must have looked like a raving idiot. How embarrassing to lose your temper so completely when everyone else was so controlled. Well, she would have to make sure it didn't happen again, no matter how angry she got. She stubbornly wiped tears from her cheeks and eyes.

But, Julie was angry. Very angry. Angry with God. No, she thought, I can't be angry with God, that's wrong. God didn't do this. I did. The tears fell unceasingly from her eyes. Sobs wracked her body as she bent over the table to put her head on her folded arms and surrender to her raging emotions.

Sometime later, when the tears slowed and her breathing became more relaxed, she began again to try to work things out. *O.K., Lord, I know I'm the one who started all this. I wanted a baby so badly that I took the opportunity and convinced myself that it was You Who was directing me. It was wrong. There should have been another way. I should have waited longer on your answer. It's just. . .I love her so much. . .* Julie broke into tears again. Her beautiful, beloved Kathy. She just couldn't give her up. And, Rick. What kind of pain had she brought into his life? Would the two of them ever forgive her for the turmoil that lay ahead? The ringing phone sobered her.

"Julie?" David asked.

"Yes, David." She must really sound awful, she thought. She cleared her throat. "I'm sorry. I'm a little hoarse this morning."

"Is Rick there?" he asked.

"No. Rick had a sales appointment this morning. He should be back early this afternoon." She paused. "David, are you going to help us?"

"Carol and I spent a good part of the night talking this over. I could be in a lot of trouble, and I could get in deeper by helping you. But, knowing what you and Rick went through trying to start a family, we can sympathize. We are in that position ourselves right now. Add to that our feelings about abortion and you have our answer. Yes, we will help as much as we can."

"Oh, David, thank you. I can't tell you how relieved I am. I don't know where we would have turned if you had said no."

"Julie, one thing. You are going to have to be absolutely honest with me. I need to know everything about this case. If you lie to me, or pad the truth, I'm out."

"I understand. I'm sorry." Julie couldn't risk saying anymore the tears were falling again.

"Have Rick call me. This is not going to be easy, Julie, but we'll give it a good run. I'm not sure we have much legal ground to stand on, but maybe the fates will intervene and be on our side."

"Not the fates, David, God," Julie answered automatically. Why did she say that, she wondered as she put the phone down? She didn't think she really meant it. Maybe everything did depend on fate. Maybe everything was only coincidence. Whatever, David's phone call had given her new hope. A shower and fresh clothes began to sound good.

Not a cloud in the sky, thought Sebrena, as she bounded out of bed and crossed to the window to greet the new day. Wynne had already left for the office. He seemed all business this morning. Nothing like he was last night. But then, she always knew how to get him to relax and take his mind off his problems. Sometimes it almost seemed too easy. She smiled. And men think they possess all the power in the world. He had promised to begin looking into the legal avenues to follow in their case against the Sierras. He was wonderful. Certain of his love, she knew he wouldn't deny her anything.

What had that preacher said yesterday? "Ask and ye shall receive." Well, God, if you are there, I'm asking, she half-heartedly prayed. Then, feeling silly, she turned away from the window. She'd gotten everything she'd wanted before without praying, why start now? Everything, that is, except her two children from Harry. Maybe things would be in her favor this time with Kathy. She'd made a good start. After all, hadn't she been good and gone to church yesterday? A crooked smile erupted. Maybe a little prayer would help. She'd try it out, later. For now she just wanted to luxuriate in her feelings of triumph.

She stood in front of the mirror, running a brush through her long dark hair. The soft billowy curls floated around her face. The look on Julie's face yesterday had told it all. She had them right where she wanted them. They were scared. They knew the scales were tipped in our favor. Wynne's influence and money. The law. And, maybe even Kathy. The child did seem pretty taken with the house and all her new toys. Certainly, if given the choice she would prefer to live here rather than in that dump on the other side of town, Sebrena thought.

"And we want to tie together the idea that both the firemen and their dalmatian have to have healthy diets to perform their jobs well. Wynne are you with me?" Ty Anderson felt like he'd been talking to himself. Obviously whatever was bothering his partner was enough to totally distract him from their new dog food campaign.

"I'm sorry Ty," Wynne said shaking himself back to the business at hand. The events of the weekend kept crowding into his mind. He knew when he'd married Sebrena life would be full of surprises, but he never expected any like this. "I just can't seem to concentrate this morning. I have some personal business on my mind."

"I can see that. Anything I can help with?" Ty offered.

"No, thanks. I appreciate your offer. I think I'm going to have to work this out on my own." How could he begin to tell Ty? He didn't understand it all himself. A daughter. He had a daughter. He wasn't sure he was pleased with the news. Obviously Sebrena had felt she was giving him some sort of gift. It was like the green sweater she'd given him on his birthday. He didn't like the feel of the wool but he wore it anyway because he didn't want to disappoint her. He loved her too much.

"Can I go ahead with the ads?" Ty kept interrupting Wynne's drifting thoughts. "We really need to get this off the board and running."

"Sure, I trust your judgement. You have a great eye for that side of our business."

"Are you saying I know a real dog when I see it?"

Wynne smiled as his partner backed out the door with his portfolio in hand. He leaned back in his chair and blankly contemplated the ceiling above. How would he have reacted, he wondered, if she had told him she was pregnant from the first. He wanted to imagine himself a knight in white armor, rescuing her and his child from her fanatical husband, but truthfully, he had spent that time in Europe trying to decide if being involved with a married woman was such a good idea. In the end, though, he had decided that there might not ever be another woman in his life as exciting or beautiful as Sebrena. He had decided to chance being hurt and press her to get a divorce and marry him.

He shifted his chair around and turned to gaze out his office window into the deep blue sky. To be sure, there had been some serious accusations made yesterday. Wynne was still confused. Sebrena had not done much to clear up the confusion.

"Dr. Erving was just a close friend," Sebrena had insisted when he had questioned her about Julie's comments. "He was my doctor, but he became a good friend by listening and encouraging me through some of the rough times I had with Harry. We were on a first name basis. If Julie thinks that everyone who is on a first name basis is sleeping with that person, then the whole world is sleeping around."

Wynne faintly remembered meeting the doctor once in a restaurant. He remembered because he had been a little embarrassed about how Sebrena had gone on and on expounding upon his accomplishments in business and politics. She had even bragged about his income. Well, if he were just a good friend and knew about Harry, she was probably just very anxious to let him know she had found someone better.

But, what if Julie was telling the truth? What if there had been a relationship with the doctor? What if they did get custody of Kathy? What if the media makes a circus out of this in the middle of the election? What if, what if, what if. What if I got some aspirin? Would it make this headache go away?

"Marge, you have any aspirin out there? I can't find any in my desk." Wynne let up on the intercom button so Marge could answer.

"Sure do. Be right in." Count on Marge to be prepared and have everything under control.

Wynne opened his appointment scheduler. He began to scan what was arranged for the next few weeks in hopes of freeing up more time for the legal problems they were about to face. Marge knocked gently before opening the door and bringing in a glass of water with two gel tabs. She set the glass and aspirin next to the photo of Sebrena and Wynne at Bar Harbor, smiled and went back to her desk.

As Wynne reached for the glass, he studied the picture. He imagined Kathy in the photo with them. A family man. Not a bad image for a politician these days. But if he wasn't careful, the image could blow up. He had to find a way to get this settled quietly.

"Marge, could you get Ed Kaplan on the phone for me?" Ed was the company lawyer, but he had promised to look into the situation and find some legal help. There had to be a way to do this quietly. There just had to.

"Will do. There's a Mike Boston from the News Herald on line two. Says he wants to set up an interview with the future state senator. Do you want me to fit him into your schedule?"

Wynne's mind raced over the possible consequences of meeting with a news reporter right now. Could he know about Kathy? "Set something up but put him off for two weeks. Tell him I'm going on vacation or a business trip or something. You're good at that, Marge. Thanks."

No, he couldn't possibly know. The Sierras never contacted the media. Still, what would happen if the proverbial fan spread the news?

"...In all thy ways acknowledge Him and He shall direct thy paths. Proverbs 3:5 and 6," Reverend Simon finished quoting. "It seems to me that's about all I can give you for right now, Rick."

Rick sat in the chair across the desk from his pastor. He was slouched to one side, his elbow propped on the armrest and his head cradled in his hand. He needed some guidance , some counsel, just a good listening ear, and the first person he had thought of was Pastor Simon.

"I'm just so confused. I don't know which way to turn. If it were a situation that only affected me or just me and Julie, I wouldn't have such a hard time. But this is Kathy's life we're talking about. Would it be better for her to be with Sebrena? I don't know."

Pastor Simon leaned forward. He bowed his head for a moment. His heart was breaking for this young man he had come to know and love. The Sierras had been very faithful in their church attendance but they had not become involved with the other families in the congregation. They had always seemed to be loners and yet hungry for companionship. Now he understood why.

He lifted his glasses slightly and wiped his moist eyes. With a burden like this, they couldn't afford to get too close to anyone. Being close to others would have jeopardized the secret they held. There had been many secrets revealed in this office in the fifteen years he had served as pastor, but never one quite as complicated or unusual as this.

"I sympathize with you, Rick," Pastor Simon finally said. "But I don't have any answers. I'm not a lawyer. I don't know where you stand legally. I'm sure you'll find that out soon enough. I can't tell you that you were right or wrong in how you acquired Kathy. I wish I could. A clear answer would be easier to deal with. I can only say that I love you and know that God loves you, right or wrong. He loves that little girl of yours too, and we need to keep her before Him. Why don't we spend some time in prayer, keeping an open heart and mind to His leading and let Him direct our paths."

Together they knelt in the small office of the church joined in the knowledge that God was the only solution when it seemed like none existed.

Eight
The Summons

"Well, here it is," Rick said somberly. He handed Julie the legal documents. "So this is what a summons looks like. I hope David has everything ready for court."

"It's happening so fast," Julie said. "What if we lose? How are we going to go on without her? What'll we do?" Julie collapsed in Rick's arms weeping.

"O.K. Enough," Rick said straightening Julie and taking a step back to look into her eyes. "Where's that gutsy lady who saved this child's life to begin with? You were strong then. You can be strong now. I'm scared too, but we have each other and together we can face anything—even this."

Julie rallied. Yes, she must be strong. Strong for Rick and Kathy. In one respect, she was thankful that Wynne Warner had political ambitions. David had told them of the pressure the Warner lawyer was putting on to settle the case out of court. He kept using scare tactics, threatening to make a criminal case out of it.

"I don't think we have to worry too much about that," David had said when they met to go over details. "Warner's political ambitions couldn't take the scandal and sensationalism that a public trial would produce. We settled on a closed hearing before a judge. That will keep the news hounds at bay and save us all a lot of grief, especially Kathy."

"That's a relief," Julie replied, "But what about those political connections with judges in the area? What if we draw one that knows him and favors him?" She shuddered. She didn't want to consider the possibilities.

David took her hand. "Just pray that God gives us one who has a deep sense of fairness and will not prejudge either side."

Judge Helen Belmonte hung her black robe over the hook behind her office door. It had been a long day. She felt drained. Lately, the divorce and custody cases depressed her more than usual. The doctor had an answer for her, postpartum blues. How could you have postpartum blues when you didn't actually deliver a baby, she thought bitterly as she set her large frame down into her padded swivel desk chair. The miscarriage had been extremely difficult for Helen. She had only been two months pregnant, barely enough time to know there was a life growing inside and yet, long enough for her body to begin hormonal changes. She wasn't a little wisp of a woman. She was a strong, black woman. Tall and big boned, she carried herself with a stately air of dignity. Dressed in her black robe, she was as imposing as any man who sat on the bench. She had the body to carry children, at least that's what her husband had told her. How could her body have betrayed her?

She glanced at the picture of Frank and their year old son. Guilt knifed through her again. She hadn't wanted another baby—not yet. There had been pills to prevent pregnancy. Then pills to get pregnant. Then more birth control pills that weren't worth the money they paid for them. Nothing ever seemed to work the way you wanted it to when you wanted it to. By some manifestation of bad luck, she had managed to get pregnant. Her career was just starting to roll again since she'd had Jeremy, and she feared another baby would slow things up again. She had even considered abortion. Hence, the guilt that hovered over her now. Was it God's way of repaying her for wanting to abort the life within her?

"You're a healthy young woman. At 33 you still have a few good child bearing years ahead of you to finish your family." The doctor had tried to bolster her spirits. "After all, nature has a way of taking care of its mistakes. This just wasn't meant to be."

Why would God give me another child and then take it away just when I decide I really do want it? Helen pushed her short curly black hair off her forehead and leaned back closing her eyes for a moment. She had to work through this. She had to get her personal grief out of the way if she was going to make any intelligent decisions in the lives of others.

"Oh, excuse me," said Ray as he entered the office. "I thought you were still in court."

"It's all right, Ray," she said smiling weakly at him. Ray was an efficient law clerk. He was finishing law school, but unsure of whether or not he wanted to go on to take the bar or to teach and write in the legal field. He was also a very caring person. He had seen her through some rough cases and had sympathized with her as she had agonized over some difficult decisions.

At first, Ray hadn't liked the idea of working for a woman. She had just been elected to juvenile court and was the only one who did not have a law clerk in her office. He soon grew to have nothing but complete respect and admiration for her. She didn't treat him as a "gofer". While he realized he still had a lot to learn, she never put him down. He knew his thick glasses perched on an all too thin and long nose in the middle of a small face that topped a body which seemed to have grown in all the wrong proportions didn't earn him much respect from others. But Helen had looked beyond that and found the quick wit, the storehouse of knowledge, and the dedication that he had to offer and praised him for it. She had a knack for looking past the surface and into a person's soul.

"What do you have for me?" Helen asked noticing the papers in his hands.

"It's a case you've drawn. I'm afraid it's another sticky custody case and extremely unique. But, I'll let you discover that for yourself. Don't want to prejudice the judge," he said winking. It was a little reference to the discussion they had one day about prejudice and how Ray felt people always judged him incapable because of his appearance. She had asked him if he would rather be black and a woman and a discussion had ensued over who received the greater injustice. She had told him how difficult it still was as a black woman when it came to politics. She hated the way people wanted favors in return for support for your campaign, that "good ole boy" networking. She wanted to make it on merit alone, on her own record, her own values, not on who she rubbed elbows with at the party conventions or caucuses. The sharing of personal hurts and disappointments had strengthened the bond between them.

"Thanks, Ray, I think," Helen said. He set the papers on her desk wishing there were some way he could lift her mood more.

"Why don't you call it a day," he suggested. "I'm the only one who gets time and a half around here. Go home."

"Good advice. Maybe, with my feet up, a nice cup of hot tea and my fuzzy robe, I can face another case. Unique, huh? You're not going to give me more of a hint than that?"

"Nope. That would be like filling you in on a movie you're going to before you buy the ticket. See you in the morning." He backed out the door and gave a little salute before closing it.

"In re Kathy S.," Helen read aloud. Warner. That name struck a familiar chord. Of course, he was this district's party candidate for the state senate. She remembered being told it would be prudent to hand out flyers for re-election at his fund raising spaghetti dinner. She had met him only briefly. He probably won't even recognize me. She rose to pile her homework into her briefcase and sighing, turned out the light before leaving.

Wynne Warner sat at his desk in the den thumping the eraser end of a pencil against his squared jaw. He waited for his lawyer to finish the amenities with his secretary and make his way into the office. Were his worse fears about to be realized? Ed had been very mysterious.

"Wynne," Ed began. "I don't like having to tell you this, but you did ask me to find out as much as I could."

"That's right, Ed," Wynne replied steeling himself for the worst.

"First of all, we did get the deposition from Dr. Erving and he stands by what the hospital records indicate. He claims Sebrena miscarried and delivered a stillborn child." Ed paused and shook his head.

"And you don't think so?" Wynne asked hesitantly.

"No. I think he's trying to save his own hide. I think he's covering something up. Either it truly was an abortion attempt or he screwed something else up that he doesn't want coming out in the wash. And there's more." Ed looked at Wynne trying to decide if he was ready to hear the rest.

"Go on," Wynne prompted. It was like getting a tooth pulled. He wanted it over with.

"There was common knowledge in the good doctor's office that Sebrena was more to him than just a patient. They were seen together in restaurants and on one occasion, Sebrena was seen leaving the doctor's apartment at an odd hour. I'd say there's substantial evidence to indicate a strong relationship there without having actual pictures of the bedroom."

Wynne used some expletives he hadn't conjured up in a while. "Is there anything else?"

"Yes, unfortunately. We have a lady who worked in admissions that night that Kathy was born. She claims that Kathy was admitted at one in the morning but your wife wasn't admitted until three. Both had Erving's name as the admitting doctor. If it had been a pure and simple miscarriage, the admitting papers would have been filled out first on Sebrena, not Kathy.

"The other bit of information we picked up from the hospital records shows Dr. Erving's signature on a requisition form for the saline solution used in abortions. Now, we can't prove that he used it for Sebrena but, Dr. Erving was not on record for having performed any abortions at that hospital before and no record of any since."

Wynne's eyes closed and his head fell into his hands. Ed didn't know what to do or say. He knew the bottom of Wynne's world was falling out and, from here, it would be one giant roller coaster ride. Mumbling an apology, he put his papers back into his briefcase and excused himself from the room.

A sob racked Wynne's body when the door closed. He wanted to feel anger over being betrayed. He wanted to rage. Instead he just felt crushed, devastated by the actions of the woman he loved so very much. Wynne was only a social drinker, but right now the small liquor cabinet in his office seemed a good refuge. He took a deep breath and buzzed Marge.

"Marge, please call my wife and tell her I'll be late tonight. Put the answering machine on and you can leave. We're done for today." He slowly rose and walked to the cabinet. While pulling his tie off and unfastening his top two shirt buttons, he reached for the scotch. Or, should I try the bourbon, he thought. He grabbed both.

Kathy hugged Wilbur in her sleep. She loved that Pound Puppy more than any other animal or creature among her stuffed collection. Maybe it was because Wilbur had to be "adopted" and Kathy related to that since she knew she was adopted, Julie thought. Julie moved to tuck the covers gently around the two of them.

When Julie had told Kathy about adoption and the fact that she was adopted, she had made up a story about a young girl who couldn't care for a baby and had to find a good home with loving parents. She hoped now she would never have to change that story. How in the world would she ever tell Kathy the truth?

"Please, Lord," Julie prayed quietly, "help me to know how to deal with this. Tell me what to say to Kathy. I've just botched everything up so badly. She'll hate me for lying to her. Please, don't make me have to tell her the truth."

"I think we owe her the truth," Rick said softly in Julie's ear. She jumped. She hadn't heard him come in.

"She'll hate us."

"I don't know about that. We did save her life. Someday she'll be grateful for that." They stood together, Rick behind Julie, his arms around her, and watched Kathy's even breathing, her sweet face reflecting the peace of childhood.

"Julie, we need to pray together tonight," Rick said as they descended the stairs and headed for the comfort zone of the kitchen. The kitchen, the heart of their home, was where major decisions were made, disagreements were smoothed out and, many times, where they sought out help for the spiritual struggles within.

"Tomorrow is going to be a rough day. We haven't prayed together in quite a while. I miss that. I need you as a prayer partner, Julie, as well as my wife."

Julie looked up at him. Her eyes glistened. She nodded her head and they sat at the table, joined hands and hearts as they reached inward and upward for strength.

Wynne was wishing they had put the master bedroom on the first floor like the architect had suggested. He wasn't sure he had the strength to make it up the stairs to shower and change. He had spent the night sleeping off the effects of a scotch and bourbon mixture. It had taken a lot before he had finally passed out. Now he knew why he was only a light social drinker. The hangover was agonizing and the problems were still with you when you sobered up.

As he quietly passed the bed, Sebrena moved and sighed but didn't seem to be awake yet. He stood for a moment looking at the beautiful face, the silky dark hair. How could she have deceived him? He hated himself for being such a fool more than he hated what she had done.

He carefully closed the bathroom door not wanting to disturb her. He stripped and started the shower. He had barely begun to lather up, when the door opened and a soft, warm body pressed against his back. Sebrena gently took the soap from his hand and began to slowly move her hands over his shoulders and down his back, stopping to caress those familiar areas she loved the most. He felt himself giving into the pleasure but then a cloud descended and he turned abruptly, causing water to spray into her eyes.

"Oooh, that wasn't nice!" she exclaimed startled by his reaction.

"Sebrena, I'm not in the mood for this right now. You and I need to have a long talk and get some things straightened out." He pushed open the door and stepped out, grabbing his towel and wrapping it around him.

Sebrena turned off the water and stepped out just behind him, her hair dripping, forming a puddle on the floor. "What do you mean? I'm not angry about you're staying out all night. I would rather you sleep at the office when you have to work that late than to risk the drive home and fall asleep at the wheel."

"You trust me enough to think that I spent the night at the office. . .alone?"

"Yes, dear. Is there any reason I shouldn't?" she said trying to get close enough to put her arms around him. Wynne kept backing away.

"What if you found out I was lying to you? What if I were seeing someone at the office? What if you found out that what you knew about me before we were married was all a big lie?"

Sebrena's face began to register fear. She reached for a towel. What was he getting at? Was this about him, or me, she wondered. "What's wrong?" she asked as she searched the bloodshot eyes and puffy face for an answer.

"Let's get dressed," he said, "We can talk about this over some tomato juice and coffee. I need some aspirin too." He headed for the closet.

Sebrena grabbed a second towel for her wet hair and followed Wynne, her heart racing. This is it. The moment of truth. But which version of the truth was going to work best this time? She had to think.

Nine

The Truth?

Wynne added salt and pepper to his tomato juice and began to stir it slowly. He wished the aspirin would start to kick in so he could think clearer. Sebrena was pouring herself a cup of coffee. Wynne looked at her smooth, sensual curves that were accented by the draping of her silky robe over a still moist body. He remembered the first time he had made love to her.

She had shown up at his door with the campaign fliers he needed for his canvassing of the homes in his district. He had been running for state representative that year from a district in the northern part of the state and she worked feverishly as a volunteer in the campaign office, making phone calls to solicit votes. When Wynne realized the flyers he needed for canvassing had not been printed up, she graciously volunteered to run them off and deliver them in person.

"Thanks," he said when she appeared at his door. He realized again how pretty this woman was. "I'm just about ready to start out for all the handshaking and baby kissing." He fumbled with his tie.

"You can just put them over there," he said nodding to a desk already overloaded with papers and poster board.

"Here, let me help you with that," she said stepping close to him. He breathed in slowly and deeply, inhaling the mystical aroma of her scent. Just as he felt himself getting lost, she patted the knot of his tie and stepped back.

"There, Mr. Representative, you are now ready to meet your constituents."

"Thank you, Sebrena. It is Sebrena, right?"

"Yes. How nice of you to remember," she said looking deeply into his eyes. "Would you like some help passing those out? That's an awfully big stack for one person to tackle."

"Well, that would be great." He tried not to appear too eager. "But, I know you've already put in a lot of time today. I wouldn't want to monopolize your time." He was feeling like the water boy for the football team who just got noticed by the cutest cheerleader on the squad.

"Nonsense. You are my man, my champion. I want to do all I can to encourage you. Support you. Your campaign, I mean." She turned a little pink at the cheeks and quickly looked down. "I do have the rest of the afternoon and evening free and I'd love to help."

"I guess I can't turn my back on my most loyal supporter," he said putting a finger under her chin and lifting those penetrating eyes back up to meet his. "Let's get rolling."

They had spent the late afternoon and early evening ringing doorbells and handing out flyers. Once or twice she had to wait for Wynne to catch up to her because people would bend his ear over their particular concern of state government. He had tried to coax her into going to a nice restaurant for dinner, but she had insisted that a bottle of wine and a great submarine from the neighborhood deli consumed in front of his fireplace in the apartment would be wonderful. The fire warmed them, the food and wine satisfied the hunger, but the atmosphere and the warmth of her nearness caused Wynne to grow bold. Sebrena didn't resist, even when his embraces became more insistent.

They spent a wonderful time exploring each others pleasures in the flickering light of the fire.

It wasn't until after the election that he had discovered she was married. He felt like he had lost twice. He couldn't be involved with a married woman, not if he were going to pursue this crazy political rat race he aspired to. That was why, when the opportunity had presented itself to make the trip to Europe, he had gone. He had needed space to think things through. If he wanted her, he would have to consider the children too. He wasn't ready for an instant family at that point in time. He didn't know if he were ready for an instant family now, especially under these circumstances. Sebrena turned to bring her coffee to the table and sit across from him. He concentrated on the tomato juice before him.

"What's going on, Wynne?" Sebrena asked keeping her hands firmly gripped on her cup. She was afraid to let go and have him see that she was shaking.

"I don't know where to begin. I have to ask you some questions about what happened before we were married, and I need straight answers. Those answers are necessary if we are to continue to pursue Kathy's custody, for that matter, if we are going to continue to pursue a marriage."

"What questions, sweetheart? What in the world has someone been telling you? Are you questioning my love for you? You know I love you as much as life itself. I will do anything for you." Sebrena stopped at that. Her philosophy was never to volunteer more than was asked for in a situation like this. She waited for Wynne to continue.

"First of all, did you really think you were miscarrying or were you attempting to abort Kathy?"

Sebrena sighed. Well, she thought, here goes. "I'm sorry," she said, her eyes tearing on cue. "I didn't know how to tell you this. I was sure you would hate me. I knew when you went to Europe, you weren't ready to take on kids, especially Harry's, but then I knew that Harry would never give the kids up if I asked for a divorce. I found out I was carrying your baby and I was afraid you wouldn't want me with a baby too. Dr. Erving was willing to try the abortion for me and label it a miscarriage so that Harry wouldn't kill me over it. I didn't know he'd never done an abortion before and I surely didn't know he would ruin my chances of having any more babies."

"You didn't have much faith in me. How could you have been so sure I wouldn't have welcomed my own child?"

"I'm sorry. Harry kept harping on me when he found out I was pregnant. I was so crazy I couldn't think clearly."

"So, Dr. Erving was gracious enough to attempt the abortion. Was that in return for the favors you were doing for him?"

Sebrena recoiled. Wynne's sarcastic attitude was out of character for him. She tried to look offended and hurt as she asked, "What do you mean?"

"Obviously, from what Ed has learned, you were most likely having an affair with Dr. Erving. You were seeing him more than just at your scheduled appointments." Wynne's anger was growing. He stared fiercely at her.

"How could you think that!?" Sebrena whined. "I was desperately in love with you at that point. I didn't even let Harry touch me. I was hoping beyond hope that you would return, take me in your arms and I could put my miserable existence behind me." She began to sob.

"Then how do you explain being with him outside the office?"

Sebrena was doing her best to keep sobbing while she allowed the thoughts to whir in her head trying to pull the right combination out to win. Wynne got up to pour another cup of coffee giving her a moment longer to think.

"I was suicidal. Dr. Erving kept insisting that I see someone but I knew Harry would have a fit, and I didn't like the idea of spilling my life story to a total stranger. Dr. Erving arranged time for me to come and talk with him and try to sort things out in my head."

"And this included dinner at a restaurant?"

"Sometimes Dr. Erving's schedule was so heavy that he invited me to join him for dinner just so he would have a chance to eat. He really was helpful. I don't think I could have gotten through that rough time without him, but that's all it was. A doctor helping a patient. Once he knew what my life was like, when I decided on the abortion, he wasn't hesitant to help."

Wynne struggled. Was she telling the truth? Was he looking for the truth or a way to excuse her? He was torn. What was making him so angry, the fact that she was admitting to the abortion or that she might be lying about Erving?

"Why did Erving say Kathy was stillborn? Why didn't he just tell you she was alive then and be done with it?"

"I told you I wasn't very emotionally stable at the time. He probably didn't want to push me over the edge. As it was, he had me knocked out. He didn't want me to know what was going on. He said partial birth abortions weren't an easy procedure for anyone, and he didn't want me aware of what was happening."

"What do you mean 'partial birth abortion'? Do you know what that is? They take the baby out in pieces. It's one of the most disgusting things our government has ever allowed."

"I didn't know that's what it meant. I. . .I. . .I was confused. I needed you and you weren't there. I needed your arms around me. I needed your wisdom. I needed your love. I still do. Please, Wynne, forgive me. If I had known it would cause you pain I never would have done it. I love you more than life. Besides, Kathy's not dead. She's alive." Sebrena rose from her chair and tried to put her arms around him. "It's meant to be. You. Me. And Kathy."

Wynne broke her hold on him and stormed out of the kitchen, through the foyer and out the front door. He had no idea where he was going. He just knew he had to walk. Had to move away from her. Had to have space, air, time.

Sebrena looked around her spacious kitchen. The light oak cabinets and white counters gave the room a bright look even on a dreary day. She loved the big window over the sink where she could look out into the trees and watch the birds and the squirrels at play. The breakfast nook was cozy and comforting. Was she about to loose it all?

With her head bowed, she gave into the emotion she had held back. She allowed herself a few moments of pity. Then, slowly she raised her head, held her breath for a moment and let it out slowly. No, no pity. She had made her choices. They weren't all bad and she had done what needed to be done to get the man she truly did love with all her heart. She had faith in that love. He would come back and she would convince him that Kathy was theirs and they would be a loving family, headed for great things.

Wynne suddenly realized he was huffing and puffing. His heart was trying to pound through the walls of his chest. He slowed down. A heart attack now would not be good. He had reached the little park in the center of their community. Thankfully, it was not a cold day. In his haste to get out of the house, he had neglected to grab a jacket. He walked to a wooden bench and sat with his head in his hands, elbows resting on his knees.

Think, Wynne, think. He told himself. Think with your head and not your heart, or any other parts of your anatomy. That's what started this whole affair. You couldn't pass up a beautiful woman, even though she was unavailable. No, that's not fair. I'm in love with her. If I didn't love her, this wouldn't cut so deeply. But, how do I resolve this? Do I take her at her word? She is vulnerable. That's part of what makes her so attractive. Brings out the stinking protector in me. I know Harry was a jerk and losing her kids was a real blow to her. She gave them up for me. How could she ask for an abortion though? I can't imagine being that desperate, but then, I don't know what it's like to carry a baby inside either. God, what a jerk I am. If I would have made my mind up sooner about her and not gone traipsing off to Europe, this never would have gotten so complicated.

He could feel himself begin to calm down. So, O.K., maybe Erving did play psychiatrist. Sebrena did have a way of getting people to sympathize with her and agree to doing it her way. He should know that by now. If she felt desperate and cornered, she may not have been thinking rationally about the abortion. People did strange and sometimes awful things when they could see no other way out of their situations. If anyone were to blame for the situation they were now in with Kathy, it was Dr. Erving. He should have had enough professionalism to make her seek the right kind of help and insist upon it. And he certainly shouldn't have tried an abortion if he didn't know how to do it right. Then there was the matter of letting the Sierras go off with Kathy. Something really smelled rotten there. Wynne's anger began to shift to the doctor and the Sierras and away from Sebrena. He knew he was probably making excuses for her, but he didn't care. He knew one thing for sure and that was that he loved her and wanted her.

"Hey, mister, could you move your foot for a minute, please?" Wynne was startled by the young voice of a little girl about Kathy's age. She was standing in front of him holding a fistful of brightly colored fall leaves.

"Honey, don't bother that man," her mother called from across the path. "I'm sorry she's being a pest."

"But I want the red one under his foot," the little girl protested.

Wynne reached down and pulled the slightly damp crimson leaf from his under his shoe. "Here you go," he said with a smile. The curly haired girl responded with a grin that lit up her face. She thanked him and skipped off to her mother and the two continued down the path, stopping to pick up another fall treasure here and there to add to their collection.

Maybe a daughter isn't such a bad thing. A little soft bundle of love to curl up in my lap and look at me like I was the most important thing in her life. A family man. Yes, I could see myself walking in those shoes. My two best girls at my side at inauguration. Wynne's step was much lighter heading back to the house and there was even the beginning of a warm fuzzy smile on his face. The battle would not be easily won, but he loved a good fight.

Mike Boston waited for Wynne to go into the house. The hopeful congressman certainly looked harried this morning. His clothes belied the possibility of this being his usual exercise routine. Something had sent him out of the house dressed for the office not a brisk walk around the block.

Boston looked at his watch. "Well time enough," he said. Opening the door, he grabbed his notepad with one hand as he climbed out of his 4-wheel drive jeep and headed for the Warners' front door. He hoped Wynne wasn't a violent man. The questions he wanted to ask him would certainly test any man's patience, especially one with an eye for political office.

Ten

The Hearing

Ray sat across from Helen as they sipped their traditional morning cup of coffee before court was to begin. The sun coming in the window revealed in slats of hazy light the particles of dust from all the law books and papers that had been shuffled and reshuffled. Ray had just finished writing down a list of judgements and precedents that Helen had given him to look up. He'd have a busy morning to be sure. There were many on her list that he had not already considered for the upcoming cases of delinquency, custody or guardianship battles and the general collection of human ugliness they dealt with each day. They worked together so well now that he was able to second guess her and often researched successfully ahead of her requests.

"Well, as usual you've done my homework for me." Helen smiled, referring to the pile of documents and books before her. Ray was a terrific asset to her, especially now when it seemed that her personal life kept interfering with her professional duty.

"You weren't kidding yesterday when you said this In re Kathy S. case was going to be unusual." Helen set her cup down carefully between folders and open books on her desk. "This is the stuff they make HBO movies out of. A nurse and a pediatric resident try to adopt a child who really wasn't born, so to speak, because apparently the procedure was an abortion and the fetus should have died. Now that she finds out, the biological mother who wanted the child dead to start with, wants custody and full documentation that she is rightfully the mother of the little girl. That poor child. It's situations like this that make me hate this job. No matter what I do, that child loses somehow."

Ray stood up, stretching like a cat in the band of sunshine falling on him and walked to the office door. "Maybe if you had the wisdom of Solomon. . ."

"What's this? Is this Ray speaking? Ray, the avowed disbeliever? Have you been reading my Bible in the closet on your breaks?" Helen's face appeared serious but the glint in her eye betrayed the good natured teasing.

"Just a matter of speech, Judge. Don't ruffle your robes. Your Bible is safe from me." He grinned and closed the door behind him.

The wisdom of Solomon. Not a bad desire. Something pricked Helen's memory of a Sunday school class she had been attending lately. The miscarriage had even persuaded her to join the ranks of the Sunday school faithful. Church was fine for worship, but she needed a little more Bible study if she was ever going to understand why God had brought such tragedy into her life. Frank had been happy. He had been constantly on her about attending Sunday school classes together. He was so excited the first Sunday that he ran and got her coffee and a donut which immediately made him the target of a lot of good natured kidding about spoiling the wife.

Last Sunday, they had studied something in the Old Testament about Solomon. What was it? She reached for her Bible behind the desk on the shelf. She had some time before the hearing. Maybe a little Bible study and prayer would be just the thing. She had been telling herself for some time now that she was going to get back to doing morning devotions. Today was as good a day as any to start.

The judge's chambers were not anything like Julie had imagined. She expected a large mahogany desk with wall to wall bookshelves lined with impressive leather bound law books. The shelves were there, but the books looked like old well worn library stock and the desk was mahogany colored but obviously laminated plastic, the same as the bookcases. Not bad looking but if it were a movie scene, it was certainly a low budget film.

Large piles of files were stacked here and there amidst open books and legal pads. Julie hoped the old saying "a cluttered desk is a sign of an organized mind" was true. Her eyes skimmed the titles of books on the shelf. She stopped. Her gaze retraced the last four or five books. Yes, it was. A Bible, just within arm's reach of anyone sitting behind the desk. Julie hoped it was a good sign.

Everyone rose as the judge entered the room. While Judge Belmonte's black robe brought with it an air of authority. Julie still felt strange that it wasn't an older gentleman, wise with age, instead of this younger woman who would be hearing their case. What was this woman like? What kind of person is she out from behind her robes? At what stage does she believe life begins? Could she abort a child?

Across the room sat Sebrena and Wynne Warner with their lawyers. Sebrena had noticed the Bible on the shelf too. She quickly assumed it was used to swear people in when they gave testimony. After all, it seemed no matter what your belief, putting a hand on the Bible meant something to people. She reached over and put her hand in Wynne's. He responded with a little squeeze. Thankfully, they had talked long into the night and he was supporting her all the way. He even seemed eager to claim Kathy as his daughter. He was excited to learn that the judge had agreed to a private hearing in her chambers. That would keep the media off for a while. He hoped the encounter with the reporter at his home had not done any damage. Boston was just fishing, he was sure. But, he was close enough to the truth to make Wynne squirm.

Ed stood up. "Good morning, Judge Belmonte. I'm Ed Kaplan and these are my clients, Mr. and Mrs. Wynne Warner." Wynne rose and extended a hand to the judge.

"It's nice to meet you again, Judge Belmonte. We met at my first fund raiser. I'm still expecting you at our clambake in two weeks with your pamphlets."

"Thank you, but we're not here to discuss politics, Mr. Warner. We can talk about that outside the court room. Right now we have a hearing to conduct."

Helen's reaction had been cool and calm, but Julie's optimism fell. They knew Wynne had connections. This is what they had feared. How much would this judge be influenced by her association with him and the political favors he could offer? The difficulty of being a black woman running for a higher position in the courts would tend to make you reach out for help wherever you could. Wynne's message had been clear.

The judge settled back in her chair comfortably as the lawyers for both sides presented their cases. Dr. Erving had refused to give a deposition until threatened and then, he had delivered one absolving him from any involvement with the adoption. As far as he was concerned the records stood and Sebrena had a miscarriage. He did not even admit to attempting to perform an abortion.

Depositions from others at the hospital, however, were damaging to his testimony and there was a great deal of evidence pointing to what had actually happened. Julie was surprised. She thought she had been more clever in covering up with the paper work. But, now, she was glad this judge would know that Sebrena never intended for Kathy to live.

It was late when the lawyers finally finished their presentations. Julie thought that they would have to wait days or weeks for the judge to decide. She began to panic when she realized that the judge was ready to make her decision immediately.

"I have had some time to review this case from the files you gave me." Helen paused and looked around at the anxious faces around her. There was never a win/win situation in a custody case, and she hated being the one who had to cause pain. But, there were children who had to come first. She drew a deep breath.

"The Sierras certainly have not followed legal procedures in this adoption, a point I should think would have been scrutinized a little more closely by their lawyer at the time." She peered at David over the top of her reading glasses. He reddened. "And, if we were to rule right now on that basis alone, this court would have to decide that Kathy is not legally their daughter."

Helen could see Julie Sierra's lip tremble as her husband reached for her hand. A twisting pang of emotional pain went through her as she imagined what this couple must be going through. The Warner's were looking very pleased at this moment.

"On the other hand," Helen continued, "Mrs. Warner obviously did not want a child at the time of Kathy's birth. Her decision to abort, in essence, was abandonment or, at least, consent to waive her rights to the fetus or child she was bearing." The smile on Sebrena's face cracked slightly. It was her eyes that told the tale though. They were fired with anger.

"I have found few precedents that can apply from previous cases in my law books to guide me in this decision. The unusual circumstances before us demand an unusual ruling." Helen paused again to look at those before her. She wanted to be absolutely sure she had their attention. She needn't have worried.

"I am issuing an interim order in this case that guardianship of the child known as Kathy Sierra will be divided between both families. She will alternate two weeks with the Sierras and then two weeks with the Warners. She will continue to attend the same school in which she is presently enrolled. You will alternate the upcoming holidays. All decisions about Kathy's well being will have to be jointly agreed upon.

"We will reconvene here the first open date on the calendar in December at which time we will review my order. I will expect briefs from both sides stating the reasons I should not declare permanent joint guardianship. Court is adjourned." Helen rose quickly and left the room before Wynne could corner her again about the election. There would be time enough later to deal with politics. She didn't want either side to feel she was swayed in her decision by political ambitions. There was silence as they all watched Helen's robes disappear behind the door to the rear.

Then conversation exploded as the families began to fight over who would have Kathy first.

"You've had Kathy the first seven years of her life. I should have her the first two weeks." Sebrena shouted. Fire in her eyes, a furrowed brow and a set jaw punctuated her opinion.

"I'm only saying that we need time to talk to Kathy. . .to help her adjust to this situation," Julie pleaded. "She has no idea what is going on. Give us the opportunity to tell her and prepare her for her visit with you. At least give us the rest of this week to let her adjust."

"Visit? She's not coming to visit. She's coming to live with us. It may only be two weeks at a time but she certainly is not just visiting," Sebrena retorted. "And that two weeks may just be stretched to total custody if we decide to appeal," she added for emphasis.

Ray, who had been sitting in the corner, came forward and suggested they use the conference room down the hall if they needed to discuss the arrangements for transferring Kathy from one house to the other. He was afraid this was going to turn into a melee and he wanted to protect Helen's office.

"Sebrena, honey," Wynne said trying to calm her down. "Let's do as the Sierras suggest and let her stay the rest of this week so they can talk to her. We can get some things ready at home in the meantime." Wynne was thinking of the rally and the opening of the new mall he wanted to attend with Sebrena. He didn't want to take a chance that Kathy would interfere with that this week. Plus, it would give them a few days to look for a nanny.

"We'll bring Kathy over right after church on Sunday," Rick offered, hoping Sebrena was softening in light of Wynne's comments.

"Fine," said Sebrena. At least that would save her another trip to church, she thought. Although, maybe all that religion had helped out. Maybe there was something to that church going, after all, the judge hadn't denied her rights to Kathy she just had to share them with Julie.

Both sides left the room hurriedly before another issue might arise. Ray held the door and closed it quickly behind the last one out. He made a large gesture of wiping "sweat" off his forehead and then headed for the back door to let Helen know they'd cleared out.

"Whew," David said when he thought they were far enough away from people not to be overheard. None of the three had noticed the man who moved into the doorway next to the water fountain where they stood. "That's the closest I ever want to come to being disbarred. I don't know if I'd recommend pursuing this through an appeal. At least with this ruling you have part custody of Kathy and will continue to have her love and be an influence in her life. There is still the possibility of criminal charges. I don't know how good a case they make without the doctor fessing up, but it certainly wouldn't be pleasant for any of us, including Kathy."

Julie's head immediately swung in David's direction, ready to respond, but she noticed Rick nodding in agreement and gave up her verbal protest. Inwardly the protest was churning. She was not going to give up this easily, even if it meant getting another lawyer because David couldn't handle the pressure. David walked with them to the parking lot leaving Michael Boston behind frantically filling the pages of his little notebook.

"How are we going to tell her?" Julie asked as they headed for Kathy's school to pick her up.

"I don't know but we need to tell her as much of the truth as she can understand."

"How is a little seven year old child supposed to understand something as ugly as an abortion?"

"I'm not too sure we should explain all that to her." Rick hesitated, knowing that Julie was struggling with what lay ahead.

"How else can we get her to understand why we did what we did?" Julie used the back of her hand to try to keep her tears from spilling over onto her cheeks.

"Before we tell her anything, we're going to pray about it. Maybe if we had done a little more praying before we jumped in and took Kathy to begin with, we wouldn't be facing this now."

"Are you blaming me?" Julie stared at Rick with a look of betrayal.

"No, I'm just as guilty of forging ahead without being sure it was what God wanted for us. I just want to be sure that He's the One leading us now." Rick watched from the corner of his eye as Julie crossed her arms over her chest and slouched against the door. This was just the beginning and the road ahead looked treacherous.

Kathy came bouncing away from the teacher on bus duty as she spotted Julie and Rick. Her pigtails were flying in the air and her books came dangerously close to spilling out of her school bag.

She's so free. So happy. So innocent, Julie thought as she opened the car door for Kathy. What is this going to do to her—dividing her between two mothers? Julie knew there would be a change, and it probably wouldn't be good.

Eleven

The Explanation

"This is tabloid stuff," roared Bart Greeley, editor of the News Herald, as he paced his office. "I can't believe you've wasted all your time running around the state gathering nothing but rumor and innuendo. You have no fact, substantiated or not. Not one. So the hearing is private. That could be for any number of reasons, the least of which would be to protect the kid. There are no criminal charges filed from either side. You've got zilch. Zero. Nada! Get your backside into something that we can print and start earning your byline." He tried to dismiss a red-faced Michael Boston with a wave of his hand and sat back down at his desk.

"I smell something here, Bart." Michael protested.

"Fact, Boston, fact. Odors just flavor the air unless you find out what's causing them. I don't want to hear another word from you unless it's printable substantiated fact."

"But there has to be an explanation for all the strange goings on between the Warners and the Sierras." He was not giving up without a fight. "And, I'm willing to bet there's a story here that's printable."

"Well, maybe you can give that explanation to the unemployment office if I don't get a story from you this week that I can print. Go find me some crime and corruption based on some old fashioned fact. You're wasting time, Boston."

Michael gave up on the argument but he wasn't about to give up on the story. He'd pacify Bart with something else while he still kept an eye on Wynne Warner and the gang. He'd find the explanation, facts and all, and produce the story he knew was there.

"Honey, Mommy and I have something to tell you," Rick began nervously. "It's about Sebrena and what is going to happen to all of us." Kathy sat wide-eyed on the sofa, a ruffled pillow crushed against her chest, staring at Rick and Julie. She was obviously confused. Julie knew it wouldn't be easy explaining the situation to Kathy and had no objections when Rick volunteered to do it.

"It's just a little white lie," Rick had said when they discussed what they would tell Kathy. "I don't want to scare her any more than she will be. Besides, there's no good way to explain what really happened." Reluctantly Julie agreed. She was just afraid it might all come back to haunt them down the road. She was relieved that she didn't have to explain as she listened to Rick continue.

"Before you were born, you were a little tiny piece of life inside Sebrena. When Sebrena realized you were growing and going to be born, she felt very sad because she knew she couldn't take care of a baby. She wanted you to have two parents to love you so she gave you up for adoption. Mommy and I wanted to love you and keep you with us and we adopted you. Do you understand what I'm saying?"

Kathy shook her head one way and then the other. She wasn't sure what he meant exactly, but she didn't like the funny way her stomach was beginning to feel.

"Do you remember when you got Wilbur? You had to sign a paper to adopt Wilbur. It's not quite the same but sort of like that. You love Wilbur very much, don't you?" Kathy confirmed that with another head shake. Her eyes became even wider. You could see her trying to assimilate and sort out the information Rick was giving her. They had talked about her adoption before but this seemed different.

"Your Mommy and I love you very much, too. But, something has happened that we are all going to have to be very brave about. Sebrena is called your biological mother, or your birth mother, because she carried you inside her tummy before you were born. Now, a judge in the court says that we have to allow you to visit with Sebrena. We have to take turns taking care of you. You get to stay with Sebrena and Wynne for two weeks and then here at home for two weeks. You're a lucky girl. You get to have two families." Rick forced a smile. It was difficult because he could feel his facial muscles begin to quiver.

"Sunday, after church, Mommy and I will take you over to the Warners' for your two week visit. Then before you know it you'll be back. . ."

"NO!" Kathy yelled. "Don't want to go. I don't like that place. I don't like Wynne . . or. . .or Sebrena." Kathy had never rebelled like this before. It startled Rick and Julie and frightened Kathy herself. But, she was more afraid of being sent away. "I wouldn't make Wilbur go away. Why do you make me go away?"

Julie reached out for Kathy but she scrambled off the sofa and ran up the stairs to her room. Julie never thought she could ever hate anyone, but at that moment she had the blackest feelings for Sebrena. She started off in the direction of the stairs. Rick stopped her.

"Let her go for a minute," he said, wrapping his arms around her. "Give her a minute to think."

"No, she needs to be held too. Listen." They could hear deep sobs coming from upstairs. Together they climbed the stairs to try to comfort their treasured love.

Sebrena was having a heyday. After the smiling and hand pumping for the mall opening she was required to attend with Wynne, she bid him a cheerful farewell and started exploring the special opening day sales in all the children's departments. Thank goodness for the special delivery service the mall offered. She'd never get it all home by herself.

"Well, Kathy, if I spoil you so be it," Sebrena said with satisfaction. Shopping was such a freeing experience, especially when you didn't have to pinch pennies. She held up on too much toy buying. After all, men liked to shop for toys. That would be a way of peaking Wynne's interest in being a daddy.

"Thank you, Mrs. Warner," the clerk said as she handed the receipt to Sebrena. "These will be delivered late this afternoon to your home. Will someone be there to receive them?"

"Yes, thank you." Sebrena replied.

"Oh, and good luck to you and your husband in the election. I think he's just the best." The clerk almost swooned as she said it.

Well, thought Sebrena as she turned to walk away, chalk another vote up to Wynne's good looks. She smiled. His very good looks.

The crying was down to a shuddering sob. The trio sat on Kathy's bed arms entwined. Without lifting her head Kathy asked, "Do I have to call her Mommy?"

"Only if you want to, Kathy." Rick swallowed hard and looked at Julie. They hadn't discussed that issue. There was a pause before she asked another question.

"What about my animals, my toys? Can I take them with me?"

"Honey, you can take whatever toys you want, but I think Sebrena will have quite a few things for you there." Julie could only imagine the kind of stuff Kathy would be offered. They would never be able to compete with the expensive articles that the Warners could afford. "Kathy, you'll only be there for two weeks. The time will go fast. You'll be in school most of the days. And then you'll be back here with us."

"Hey, are we going to get to the zoo today or not?" Rick tried to muster some enthusiasm. "We need to get our food line started to make those sandwiches."

"You're right, Dad," Julie responded trying to put some cheer in her voice. "Let's get going."

"What was the name of that hippopotamus?"

"Herman, Daddy." Kathy rolled her eyes at him, and he tickled her ribs slightly bringing up a small giggle.

They began their assembly line for fixing sandwiches. Kathy spread the mayonnaise, Rick added the bologna and Julie packed them in the bags. It was a sweet-sour feeling for all of them. A fun day at the zoo followed by separation for two weeks tomorrow after church. Julie feared for herself as much as she did Kathy. How would they all survive this?

"Hello, Kathy," Sebrena said as Julie and Rick stood in the door with Kathy's suitcase in hand. "Come and give Sebrena a hug. I've missed you."

Kathy looked at Julie. She nodded and Kathy dutifully walked to Sebrena and allowed herself to be hugged. Her eyes looked at Julie with uncertainty. Julie braved a smile to try to reassure her.

"It wasn't necessary to bring her clothes," Sebrena straightened and looked Julie coldly in the eyes. "I have plenty of nice things for Kathy here."

"I'm sure you have." Julie struggled to keep her voice even. "I thought Kathy might feel more comfortable with some familiar things."

"Fine," said Sebrena, her icy tone signifying her irritation. "We will see you in two weeks then."

Kathy ran to Julie and Rick, kissing and hugging them both. A tear trickled down Rick's cheek and Kathy wiped it away.

"See you later, Daddy," Kathy whispered, her voice quivering.

Julie could read the determination in her expression. Kathy was being brave for them. Grayness was beginning to close in on her. Julie knew she needed to leave quickly or she was going to pass out there in front of everyone. She grabbed the doorknob for strength and tugged on Rick's arm. He was right behind her offering his support as they walked to the car and got in. Rick pulled the car into the first empty parking lot they passed and they fell into each other's arms, a sick feeling of grief consuming them both.

Kathy was overwhelmed by the amount of toys and stuffed animals that filled her room at Sebrena's house. It would take her weeks to name them all. She explored the closets and found racks of dresses and outfits, price tags still attached, that made it look like a miniature children's department store.

"Well," Sebrena began impatiently, "What do you think? It's a little girl's dream come true isn't it?"

"It's nice," Kathy replied, trying to sound enthusiastic. Julie and Rick had taught her to be excited over gifts even if she didn't like them so that the gift-giver would feel appreciated. But the big a knot in her stomach gnawed at her. She felt homesick already.

"Get your things put away and come downstairs. We'll watch some TV until Wynne gets home. Would you like some popcorn?"

"O.K., I guess." Kathy turned to her suitcase on the bed and began to fumble with the latches. They snapped open just as Sebrena closed the door and Kathy jumped back, her heart pounding. She was alone. She stood in her new room, touching her old things, wondering what she had done that would make Mommy and Daddy send her away for two weeks.

She grabbed Wilbur and hugged him tightly. "I'll never send you away Wilbur. I love you." He was the best friend she had in the whole world now.

Kathy's eyes strayed over the bed and stopped on a familiar face. She was glad to see Herman again. She picked up the soft hippo and kissed him lightly on the head. "Have you been good since I've been gone?" Herman nodded yes with Kathy's help. "Good. I know we can be friends."

She looked back to Wilbur and cuddled him as she sat on the bed. "Wilbur, what's it like to be an orphan. That's what you were before I 'dopted you. What's it like to not have a mommy?" She thought for a moment. "I guess I'm lucky 'cause I got two. I just don't feel very lucky."

"Kathy." Sebrena's voice on the intercom startled Kathy. She hadn't expected the box on the wall to start talking to her. "I have popcorn all ready. Come and get it while it's still hot."

Kathy put Wilbur in one arm and Herman in the other and began her trek downstairs. Her feet felt like dead weights at the bottoms of her legs. She was still thinking about what Mommy and Daddy told her about Sebrena.

"Sebrena is your mother too," Daddy had said. But how do you get two mothers? Other kids she knew had two mothers but there was always something called a divorce where the first mommy and daddy didn't like each other and went and married other people. It was all very confusing. The smell of popcorn turned her thoughts to television.

Wynne was in the family room when Kathy entered. She looked at him uneasily. There was something about Wynne that made Kathy feel that he didn't like her.

"Hello, Kathy," Wynne said. "Come and join us for some popcorn. We were going to watch the Muppet Caper. I rented the tape for you. I thought you might enjoy it."

"I saw it," Kathy said flatly.

"Oh." Wynne was obviously disappointed but tried to move on undaunted. "Would you like to see it again?"

"I guess." Kathy sighed and sat down on the sofa facing the wide screen TV that was beginning to show the federal warning on the rented video.

"Good. Here it goes." Wynne questioned why he felt so intimidated by this child. She's only a little girl. I've taken on grown men who should have intimidated me more. It was this father thing. Am I really cut out for this? Well, maybe I can survive. After all, it's only two weeks at a time.

By the end of the movie, Wynne was sound asleep, Kathy was yawning and Sebrena was chattering endlessly about the Muppets.

Julie and Rick walked through the quiet empty house. Neither had eaten much at the restaurant. They sat in front of the television and Rick flipped through the channels. Nothing looked particularly interesting. The Sunday paper was discarded after a cursory glance through the special weekly sections.

"Would you like to go for a walk?" Rick asked, breaking the silence.

"No, I don't think so. . .unless you really want to." Julie continued to stare at the TV screen.

"I guess not." Rick pulled the ottoman over with his foot, kicked his shoes off and propped his feet up. "Want to share?" He gestured to the ottoman.

"Huh? Oh. No. Thanks. I've seen it. Coffee?"

"No. I don't think so. Thanks."

"O.K. I'll make a some." Julie got up and went to the kitchen and began the coffee pot. She returned to her seat next to Rick as it started to drip into the carafe.

"Football O.K.?" Rick asked.

"Guess." Julie shrugged.

The aroma of coffee floated from the kitchen into the living room, swirling around their heads, but the two sat silently still in the darkened room, the blue and white light from the tube flashing on their expressionless faces. The liquid in the coffee pot darkened slowly turning into hot sludge.

"Wouldn't it be wonderful to have Kathy all the time?" Sebrena asked Wynne as he stood, toothbrush in hand in front of the bedroom television set watching the news. "She's such a wonderful child. We could have lovely evenings together like this all the time. Wasn't it cozy to just sit by the fireside with our peanut butter sandwiches and chips and watch Disney as a family?"

Wynne rolled his eyes and walked to the bathroom to spit out the toothpaste. Cozy? I don't think so. Cozy is two people curled up in front of a fire. Two adult people. A man and a woman. That's cozy. He had been right. He wasn't cut out for this father thing. His Sunday evening had been intruded upon. He returned to the bedroom and climbed between the smooth sheets next to Sebrena.

"I think it's going to take some time to feel 'cozy', Sebrena. Kathy is still very strange to us and to this house." And definitely strange to me, he added to himself.

Sebrena snuggled up against his back, softly kissing his neck. "Well, you'll see. When you get used to being a father, you'll want to be a full time father. Then you'll agree with me that we need to appeal the judge's decision." Her warm breath made his spine tingle.

Wynne closed his eyes. Something about this just didn't feel right to him. He thought he wanted to be a father to Kathy but, when he was with her, he felt uncomfortable. What was this great need of Sebrena's to be a mother again? Their evenings together had been much cozier with only the two of them. He escaped into sleep.

Twelve

A Biological Father

"Mommy!"

Julie bolted upright in bed. Kathy was calling. She quickly groped her way through the bedroom into the hall where the night light led her to Kathy's room. She bent over the bed to soothe her daughter and discovered she was gone. Then she remembered.

Climbing onto Kathy's bed, Julie found Barnaby, Wilbur's counterpart. She curled up with the precious pup and laid her head on Kathy's pillow. Wilbur was gone. Julie knew Kathy would take him. Maybe she left Barnaby behind to comfort me. What was happening, she wondered? Was Kathy crying out in the night? Would Sebrena hear her? Would she be patient enough to talk Kathy through a nightmare? She ached to hold Kathy and brush her fingers through her soft hair. Quietly she sobbed into the pillow until she fell into an exhausted sleep.

Rick rolled over to turn off the alarm, reaching over the empty space where Julie should have been. He padded out into the hall scratching his head, trying to get his head cleared of sleep. As he passed Kathy's door, he saw Julie on the bed, arms wrapped around one of Kathy's stuffed animals, sound asleep. He hated to wake her and for a moment was tempted to let her sleep. But, he knew that she needed to be up soon anyway, If she didn't go to the hospital, she would mope around the house all day wondering what Kathy was doing.

"Honey." Rick gently rubbed her arm. "You have to get up for work."

"Mmhmm." Julie moaned. "I'm coming."

Rick stared at the face in the mirror, razor poised midair. He was worried. The dark circles under Julie's eyes revealed more than Julie was telling. He shuddered. If they lost Kathy for good Julie would be destroyed. If only there were some way to appeal and get Kathy on a permanent basis. But they couldn't afford to push their luck. For that matter, they probably couldn't afford the lawyer's fees. He did his best to repair the razor's damage to his face from his lack of concentration.

In the kitchen, Julie was bent over her Bible at the table. She closed the book and looked up as Rick headed for the coffee pot. "I've been thinking. Maybe there is a way around Sebrena that could get Kathy back for us."

"That would be nice but I don't see how." Rick poured his coffee and sat next to her.

"What if we were to enlist Dr. Erving's help. I'm convinced that he's Kathy's father. If that's true then we could get him to file suit for custody and have him sign custody or guardianship over to us. After all, he didn't fight me when I needed his signature on the hospital documents. If the court is so concerned about a biological parent's rights then shouldn't he be involved?"

"Whoa! This could really get complicated. Have you considered that maybe Dr. Erving might not want to assign us any rights? Or, what if the court saw that Kathy had two biological parents and split the custody between them and took us out completely? I think you're headed into dangerous territory with this. We have an agreement now that at least gives us a part of Kathy's life. I'm afraid of losing out entirely with another wild scheme."

Julie felt like she'd been slapped in the face. He was blaming her for this. He wasn't saying it outright, but she could tell by his choice of words. She had to try something. She refused to sit and let things slide by. "I got us into this. I will get us out."

"Julie, I don't want you doing anything about Dr. Erving. Leave it alone. Our arrangement will take some getting used to but we'll do it." Rick's tone was a little harsher than he intended. He left for work with an uneasy feeling in his gut.

The drive to Vernon City was taking longer than Julie remembered. Her anxiety level was rising with each passing mile. She had called in sick to the hospital when Rick was safely on his way to work. Her next call was to Dr. Erving's office.

"I'd like to make an appointment to see the doctor." Julie tried to keep her voice from quivering.

"Sure. Have you ever been to this office before?" This had to be a new receptionist or nurse. She was sweet and sounded nothing like the stern sterile nurse he used to have.

"No, I haven't."

"What would you be coming in for?"

"Just a check up. I'd like to get started on the pill."

"Well, the doctor likes to spend a little more time with a new patient. When would you like to come in?"

"If you have anything available late this morning or early afternoon that would be great."

"Oh, I don't know. Hold on a minute." Julie could hear muffled talking in the background. "You are in luck. Mrs. Arden just had her baby last night and obviously won't be coming in for her check up today. I can give you an 11:30 if that's all right."

"That's great." Julie stopped holding her breath.

"What did you say your name was?"

"It's Schaeffer. Julie Schaeffer." Julie hung up the phone, grabbed her car keys and was out the door in a flash.

She thought she had plenty of time, but now, after getting stuck in construction delays, she was getting worried. Wasn't it time to put those orange barrels away for the winter? She looked at her watch. 10:45. It couldn't be too much farther.

Dr. Charles Erving took a moment to reflect on how smooth the office seemed to be running this morning. Mrs. Arden's delivery had gone without a hitch last night. They had no delivery dates in the immediate future. Barring any unforeseen emergencies, the office should run rather smoothly the next few days. A little time off in the Bahamas to shed the ghosts of the past that haunted him lately would make him a new man.

"Dr. Erving there's a new patient in 3. She's in for birth control pills." Lily was a sweetheart. It was nice to have her in the office. Thank goodness he didn't have to have his sister working there any more. Now he only had to put up with her once a week at home. He wished she'd get a life of her own and quit trying to be his mother. She insisted on coming in to clean and restock his refrigerator every week. That was bad enough but she also took it upon herself to answer his phone and meddle in his personal business. Sister or not, he'd about severed the relationship when he caught her talking to some reporter about his position at the hospital and his stand on abortion. How he wished he'd never met Sebrena. He couldn't bring himself to fully trust another woman again.

"Thanks, Lily. Do we have any more before lunch?"

"No, doctor. Nothing until 1:30."

"Great." Charles was noting the name on the chart as he turned the knob to open the door. He entered and, without looking up, closed the door behind him. "Mrs. Schaeffer. It is Mrs.? You didn't note that on the sheet." He looked up with a smile that froze.

"Hello, Dr. Erving." Julie greeted him from across the room.

"What is this? What are doing here?" He tossed the clipboard on the counter making a loud crack.

"I need to talk to you about Sebrena and what she's done to us. I hate to involve you again but I think it's necessary for my daughter's sake."

"I have nothing to say to you. I want nothing to do with any of this. You made me jump through your little hoops before but that's it. No more."

"Dr. Erving, is there somewhere else we could talk about this. I have some very personal questions to ask you and I don't think you want them overheard."

Charles put a hand to his forehead. Every time he thought he'd buried the past, it seemed to jump right back at him. Maybe if he talked with her this last time it would be done with. "Look, I'll give you a half hour. Let me tell the others they can leave for lunch. We can have the privacy we need right here. But I'm telling you now, I don't want anything to do with you, that baby, or Sebrena ever again. Ask your questions but I'm not guaranteeing answers."

Charles explained to Lily and his receptionist that Julie was an old friend who had surprised him. Everyone was free to leave for lunch early. He and Julie were going to catch up on old times. Just to make it appear friendly, Charles poured two cups of coffee and invited Julie into his office. It wasn't long before they were alone.

He sat behind his large cherry wood desk, leaning back in his chair. If his posture intended to be intimidating, it wasn't working. Julie was determined. "Dr. Erving, I want to know exactly what your relationship with Sebrena was when Kathy was born."

"It's none of your business."

"It is if you are Kathy's father."

A small smile played across the doctor's face. "And just why would that be so important to you?"

"If you are Kathy's biological father, you have a right to say who should have guardianship over her." Julie's voice faltered a little. "I had hoped to convince you that Rick and I should be those guardians, not Sebrena."

Charles began to note that this was not the same belligerent woman he remembered in the delivery room. Although she was aggressive with her questions, the dark circles under her eyes, the quiver in her voice all indicated the strain she was under. Sebrena had struck again. A small seed of sympathy for the woman now before him and a thirst for compensation for the humiliation he'd suffered began to grow. This could be pay back time for him. He could even the score. He was torn between trying to maintain his dignity and privacy and wanting the sweet taste of revenge.

"Julie, I have spent seven years trying to overcome my feelings about what happened in that delivery room that night. It affected everything I do in my practice and my life outside the hospital. What I am going to tell you now, I will deny if you ever try to make it public. I made the biggest mistake of my life becoming involved with Sebrena and her problems. I was a fool. As a man and a doctor. I let myself believe that this woman was truly interested in me. I was foolishly in love with her. She wanted me to prove my love by performing an abortion. She told me some crazy story about her husband and that he would never let her go if she had the baby. I truly thought she would leave him for me. I'd never done an abortion before." Charles leaned forward and clasped his hands together on top of the folders on his desks.

"I knew she had lied about how far along she was. I denied it to myself. The only procedure that would have insured success was a partial birth abortion but I didn't think I could handle that so I hoped for the best with the saline. You know the rest. Actually, I felt rather relieved when you took over. I knew Sebrena didn't want a live baby. So, you did me a favor. I only wanted to protect my position at the hospital and my practice. It's been a living hell every time anything comes close to dredging that incident all up again."

Julie felt sorry for Dr. Erving. Maybe she had misjudged him. Maybe he wasn't quite the monster she had thought. "Was Kathy your child?"

"Sebrena had told me it was Harry's child, conceived before she had met me. She began treating me very differently right after the abortion. The thought crossed my mind that it might be my child and, perhaps, if it were, there might be a way to hang on to our relationship. But, the baby was too mature to be mine. I checked the records in the lab as well, the blood tests they ran on Kathy showed that she couldn't possibly be my child. It became obvious that Sebrena had led me on only for the accomplishment of her own purposes. She had used me."

Julie was obviously disappointed. "I'm sorry," she said sincerely. She had noticed a weariness creep into his voice that had softened his usual gruffness. He had shown her his vulnerability.

"Not as sorry as I am. I never told Sebrena that Kathy lived. As far as she was concerned, I had followed through with our plan to call it a miscarriage so that she could lie to her husband and try to get her divorce. I didn't realize the man she had introduced me to at lunch one day was the one she intended to marry. I truly thought she meant to marry me. So, you see Julie, I do not relish having any of this out in the open. I can't help you any more than to wish you luck."

Julie noticed his softness vanishing, being replaced by his look of professional detachment. There wasn't any thing else to ask. She had her answer. "Thank you, Doctor. I wish it had worked out differently for all of us. The only good to come of this is Kathy, and I fear for what this all will do to her now." She rose to leave. For a moment she hesitated, deciding whether to extend her hand or not. Instead she just nodded and let herself out of the office.

Charles put his head in his arms on the desk. It still hurt. Revenge would be so sweet, but there was really no way he could strike back at Sebrena but to hope that the Sierras would win out. There had never been another woman in seven years. It was too hard to trust again.

Julie drove home barely noticing anything along the way. So, who was Kathy's biological father? Wynne? Harry? Someone else? This is the woman with whom the court wants me to share Kathy? How can they do this? What makes a set of genes more important that a set of loving parents who care for and nurture a baby? To Julie's anger was added disgust. But anger and disgust were only concealing the deep pain of anguish over the awful changes that were being made in their lives.

Thirteen

Divided

Kathy dawdled over her cereal. The crunch had disappeared long ago and limp pieces of Frosted Flakes hung over the edge of the spoon, dripping milk back into the bowl. Julie noticed Kathy's pale color and the dullness of her usually bright eyes. She thought Kathy's color would improve and her sparkle return after a few days at home but it was almost time to return her to Sebrena's and she was still not herself. Julie kept feeling Kath's forehead to see if she had a fever.

"Just about time to get ready for school, Pumkin." Julie tried to sound cheerful. She wished she could keep Kathy home and just have her near all day long. Two weeks was not enough time to give her as much love as she wanted to give. Sunday would be another heart wrenching day of having to give her daughter back to that woman.

Kathy pushed her chair back and took her cereal bowl to the sink. Her head hung down as she trudged toward her bedroom to dress for school. Julie stopped her with a hug. Instead of her little arms encircling Julie's neck in an embrace, they hung limply at her sides. She stood for a moment letting Julie hug her and then pulled back to continue on.

Something is wrong with her, I'm sure of it, Julie thought. I'm going to make an appointment for a check up with Dr. Jansen when she comes home in two weeks. She must need some vitamins or something. She's certainly not our perky little girl any more. But, then, after all she's been through, what can we expect? A crash from upstairs shattered Julies' thoughts.

"Kathy, are you all right?" she yelled as she took the stairs two at a time. She rounded the door to Kathy's room just as a stuffed bunny fell at her feet. Kathy's menagerie looked helplessly back at her from various parts of the room where they had landed. One had sent Kathy's jewelry box smashing against the wall. Bracelets and necklaces lay scattered among the animals.

"Kathy, what happened? What did you do?" Julie asked anxiously. A look of rage, foreign to Kathy's face, froze Julie for a moment. She crossed the room and put her arms around the little stranger that looked like her daughter. Kathy stiffened. "It's all right, Honey. We'll clean up later. We need to get down to the car. Daddy's about ready to go."

Julie heard Rick come in from warming the car and took Kathy's hand to lead her downstairs. Her look told Rick not to ask questions. Bewildered, he dropped Julie at the hospital and took a silent Kathy to school. He continued on to the church for his weekly meeting with Pastor Simon.

Rick had agreed to meet with Pastor Simon for a time of prayer each week and came to depend upon it to get him through the tough days. Just being able to share his burden of emotions with a friend was a comfort even though the pastor didn't have any answers for him.

"I'm really worried about Julie," Rick said. "She has a lot of hate building up for Sebrena, and I think she's carrying a lot of guilt over what she's done to Kathy's life by adopting her the way we did."

"It's understandable that she would go through some very bad feelings," the pastor replied. "Just because we have a deep faith and commitment to

Christ doesn't mean we never make mistakes. And, maybe this wasn't a mistake. Maybe God wanted this all to happen. If you can just keep your eyes on Jesus—just keep looking to Him for your guidance—He will see you through this storm of emotions and pain. Don't let the pain block out His love. Keep your heart open to Him."

"I wish Julie and I could talk the way you and I do these mornings. She seems to grow more distant as the weeks pass. This morning, I know there was something going on between her and Kathy, but I got a look that told me I'd better not ask. I'm not even sure she's been spending time in her Bible like she used to."

"Rick, you need to start praying together again. The doors of communication are open so much wider when two people are praying together. That's why this time we spend together is so special. We've come to rely on each other for that deep support which comes only by praying for and with each other. Please, reach out and try."

"I will." Rick bowed his head and wiped at the corner of his eye. They prayed together in the little office, sharing each other's needs with their Savior. Rick left knowing he would need to confront Julie and feeling that it would be all right.

Sunday's morning worship service was a void to Julie. Her only thought was of taking Kathy back to Sebrena. The mountain of hate was building. That woman didn't deserve Kathy. She's nothing more than an attempted murderer. She should have been taken to court for her crime. Yes, that was it—a crime. She was a criminal. She had no right to that precious child. Her other children were abandoned so that she could go off with another man. She didn't want Kathy to love and care for. She wanted Kathy to show off. It would garner more votes for her husband with the picture perfect family featured on the front page of the newspaper. Well, I wonder how the world would respond if they knew what kind of woman Wynne Warner married.

Julie was startled when the congregation stood suddenly to begin the parting hymn. She hadn't heard a word of Pastor Simon's sermon. Red faced, she hoped no one had noticed anything strange in her expression. She knew the mountain of hate was wrong, but she couldn't move the mountain, not alone. Where was God when she needed Him? What had He revealed that gave her confidence that He was working things out? Nothing. As a matter of fact, if He'd given them the child they'd asked for in the first place, they wouldn't be in this mess now.

Julie sucked in her lip and bit down on it. She knew if she'd had her own child, Kathy never would have been a part of their lives. She never would have known the bright cheerful little bundle of joy that now sat sullenly in the back seat as they drove across town to the Warner's home.

Julie didn't go in with Kathy this time. She let Rick walk her to the door. It had been two days since she remembered Kathy saying much of anything. What was she thinking? Did she prefer the Warners to them? Was Sebrena turning Kathy's loyalty with lies? Buying her love with toys?

Rick returned to the car. There was an ocean of silence between them as they drove home and it was growing wider and deeper.

"Well, Kathy, how does it feel to be home again?" Wynne asked as they finished their Sunday dinner. He noticed that Kathy ate very little. Maybe the flu made her look so pale. He hoped not. He couldn't afford to pick up a bug now with the campaign just beginning to gain momentum.

"Honey, Wynne asked you a question," Sebrena prompted frowning at Kathy. If Wynne was going to warm to Kathy, this sullen attitude needed to change. She sensed Wynne's impatience.

"O.K." Kathy answered shrugging. "But my name is Kathleen. When I live here it's Kathleen." A mystified look passed between Sebrena and Wynne.

"Sorry, Kathleen," Wynne said emphasizing her name.

"Kathleen, why don't you go up to your room and play with the new Barbie clothes I bought while you were gone," Sebrena suggested. Wynne needed some special attention to smooth over the rejection he obviously felt from Kathy.

Kathy sauntered out of the kitchen and up to her room, pleased to be escaping more conversation with them.

"That child looks ill," Wynne said.

"She just seems a little tired. Who knows what the Sierras have kept her busy doing." Sebrena began clearing dishes from the table.

"I hope she doesn't have the flu. I hate to think of you being up all night with her."

"It wouldn't be the first time I've had to take care of a sick child. But, you're right. I wouldn't want to be up with her all night. I'd rather be in bed with you." She shot him her most seductive look. "How about a piece of cheese cake with a little strawberry sauce?" Sebrena leaned over Wynne's back and tickled his ear with her lips.

"Mmmm. Cheesecake sounds almost as delicious as you. But it looks better with strawberry sauce than you do."

"Thanks a lot," she said laughing. It pleased Sebrena to see Wynne relax now that Kathy had left the room. Some pampering and a little time to get used to being a father and Wynne would come to enjoy Kathy's two week visits.

Julie used her walk home from work to do some heavy thinking. There were some things she really needed to share with Rick, starting with the visit to Dr. Erving's office. She noticed Rick's car in the driveway as she turned up the walk to the front steps, curious to know what had brought him home early.

"What is this?" Julie asked Rick as she stood in the middle of a kitchen glowing with candlelight. The table looked like a page out of Martha Stewart's latest magazine. Two place settings of good china, silver and two crystal goblets graced the table along with fresh flowers and linen napkins. It was picture perfect and very romantic.

"Tonight my wife gets pampered to show her how much I love her." Rick put his arms around her gently for a moment and then reached for her chair. "Madame, please sit here. You will find this a most interesting and delightful culinary treat."

Rick bowed as he pulled the chair out for Julie. She curtsied politely before sitting in her designated place. It truly was a culinary delight and Julie thought better of asking what restaurant had such wonderful carry out. She sat back and let him serve. To spoil this moment would be a sin. She would wait until later to tell him about the trip to Dr. Erving's office and her other meeting. Or, maybe he didn't need to know about either one.

After their candlelight dinner with soft music, Rick led Julie upstairs to their room. More candles had been placed around the room and in the bathroom off the hall. She smiled. The thought of Rick loading his cart with candles at the store made a comical image in her mind. What was he up to now, she wondered, as he stood before her holding her shoulders.

"Now, it's time for a sensually soothing bubble bath that I will prepare for Madame to luxuriate in for as long as Madame pleases, or until I get the dishes done. If Madame would kindly remove her clothes. I will go and draw the bath." He bowed formally again.

Julie hid her giggle behind her hand. She'd never seen him this way before. Certainly he had done little romantic things through the years, surprising her with bouquets of flowers or a special gift, but this. . . well this. . .there was no way to describe it.

Rick allowed Julie some time alone in the mound of bubbles surrounded by the flicker of candlelight. It did feel so good. She rested her head against the edge of the tub, closed her eyes and relaxed, allowing her mind to slip back to those days when they had first fallen in love. Amy Grant had brought them together. Well, actually, her concert had. It was just at the beginning of her rise to stardom. She was among a collection of artists at the concert held in the college's auditorium. Rick and Julie's friends knew each other and everyone met at the hamburger hangout at the north end of campus after the concert. She couldn't believe this wonderful pre-med student was actually paying attention to every word she said. Before the evening was over, they had agreed to meet for coffee and donuts before church on Sunday. They had both been so innocent. Their love had grown so sweetly. She recalled their first kiss, stolen quickly at the door as they said good night. It had been a soft velvety kiss.

Rick brushed his lips against hers softly and she opened her eyes to see the light of the candles sparkling in his. She was caught in a moment of wonder that this man could really love her and want her this much. Her news could wait. She didn't want to ruin this.

He took her hand and helped her from the tub wrapping the large soft towel around her. Gently, he dried the smooth curves, lingering in familiar places long enough to make their breathing deepen. Brushing the ringlets of wet hair from her ears, he placed a kiss on each one. The spell was never broken as they moved slowly from the bathroom to the bed. Julie had forgotten how tender their lovemaking could be. She immersed herself in him and floated in a sea of wonder and love.

Kathy loved her Pound Puppies more than anything else. She lay back on her pillows clutching Barnaby in one and Wilbur in the other. They were the only constant thing in her life right now. They went with her to each home every two weeks. She would never leave them or make them go anywhere without her like Mommy and Daddy had done to her.

Kathy fought sleep even though she was very tired. She hated waking up in the middle of the night and not remembering which house she was in. She was embarrassed when Sebrena found her wet bed one morning. Sebrena had been very angry and she was sorry it had happened, but she couldn't remember where she was and where the bathroom should be that night. She had fallen back to sleep only to awaken to damp sheets in the morning. If she could stay awake she wouldn't forget where she was and she would be able to find the bathroom if she needed it.

Kathy's body jerked slightly as exhaustion finally caused her to drift into a fitful sleep. Barnaby and Wilbur looked a little relieved as Kathy's arms relaxed her grip on them. But soon the nightmares began.

Fourteen

Nightmares

Julie awoke smiling. The sensation felt foreign to her face. It had been a long time since she faced a new day in such a good mood. She rolled over and looked at Rick lying beside her. He appeared at peace with the world. Such a loving and caring person. She didn't deserve him but, this morning, she was not going to question her good fortune to have him. She was just grateful she did.

"Morning," Rick mumbled, his eyes still closed. She lifted herself on one elbow to kiss him.

"I was wondering if you were going to get around to doing that," he said. His eyes opened and he grinned, reaching out to draw her near.

"Thank you for last night," Julie said.

"My pleasure, Madame."

"I. . .I guess I haven't been much of a wife lately. I'm sorry. Sorry you had to go to all that trouble last night to show me."

"Hey, that's not why I did it." Rick stroked her hair and turned her head so he could look into her face. "I wanted to show you how much I love you. I wanted to make you feel special and loved and wanted and. . .and alive."

"You certainly did all that and I love you for it. I know I've been very difficult to live with and I feel awful about how I've neglected you." She paused. "I also feel awful about what I did yesterday. You're not going to be happy. I went to see Dr. Erving."

"You what!?" Rick sat up. "I told you to leave him out of this." He turned and swung his feet over the side of the bed.

"I'm sorry. I was just so sure. But, you were right. I shouldn't have gone. He can't help anyway." Julie moved to sit next to Rick. "He doesn't think he's Kathy's father. Sebrena told him it was her husband's child and she couldn't get a divorce if he knew she was pregnant. Dr. Erving regrets ever getting involved. But at least we have a better idea of what kind of woman Sebrena is, for all the good it does us. I'm sorry."

Rick sat with his head cradled in his hands a few moments. Julie stroked his back.

"Look, Julie," Rick said, tears in his eyes. He took both her hands in his. "This whole mess has been awful for both of us. But, we can't continue to push each other away, shut each other out. I've been as guilty of that as you have. Forget about Dr. Erving. Let's begin fresh with this morning. A new beginning. I'd like very much for that new beginning to include our prayer time together again. I've missed that. I need you not only as my partner in love but in prayer as well."

Julie's eyes brimmed with tears. "I need you too. I love you."

They clasped hands and began the new day with prayer. Prayer for Kathy, for the Warners, for their own renewed bond of love. Julie wept through most of it. She knew the hatred in her heart had to go. And the other secret meeting she knew she couldn't share with Rick weighed on her heart even more.

Kathy woke screaming. Wynne rushed into her room thinking she was in some sort of terrible trouble. She was sobbing uncontrollably. Wynne felt unnerved. Let's face it, he told himself, you've never been any good with weepy females. He held her hand and patted her head. Finally, she seemed to be more awake. The crying dwindled to little spasms.

"What's the matter?" Wynne asked.

"Bad dream," Kathy hiccupped.

"Want to tell me about it?"

"No, I'm O.K. now." Sharing what she couldn't understand herself seemed futile. She never knew who was chasing her or why she was falling, but, every night, it was the same and she dreaded sleep. Added to the confusion of her dreams was the bewilderment of waking up and trying to remember where she was.

"How about some breakfast? I think Sebrena has something special she's making for us. Pancakes maybe. How does that sound?" Wynne admired this little character. She sure was tough. She still trembled from the nightmare but she didn't cling to him or fish for his sympathy. She handled her own fears. Admirable.

Kathy climbed out of bed and Wynne helped her on with her pink robe. She followed him down the steps to the kitchen.

"Are we hungry this morning? Would you like two or three pancakes?" asked Sebrena reaching into the box of frozen blueberry pancakes. Without waiting on an answer she popped two pancakes on a plate and shoved them into the microwave. "Breakfast will be ready in exactly two minutes and thirty seconds. You two have a seat."

Kathy managed a few bites of her pancakes and then excused herself to get ready for school. As she trudged back to her room, she thought about the note Mrs. Katz had sent home with her yesterday.

"Please give this note to your mother," Mrs. Katz had said. Did that mean she was supposed to give it to Mommy or Sebrena? There was only one note. Maybe she should ask for another so she could give one to each of them. She'd figure it out later. Thinking made her tired.

Sebrena startled Kathy as she fumbled with the last button on her blouse. Kathy froze as she crossed the room to begin to make the bed.

"Wilbur had a accident last night," Kathy stammered.

"Don't lie to me," said Sebrena, staring down at the soiled bedclothes. "Wilbur is a stuffed animal. He can not make your bed wet. Why can't you get up and go to the bathroom like a normal child? You are too old to be bed-wetting."

Sebrena had lost all patience. Another wet bed incident was just too much to take. She ranted and raved at Kathy while she threw sheets and bedclothes around uncovering the mattress to air it out. Kathy sat in the corner, school bag on her lap, and watched Sebrena fuss. She decided to give the note to Mommy.

Julie smoothed the covers on Kathy's bed. Her little darling would be home again soon. Maybe this arrangement was workable. While Kathy was with the Warners, she could spend the two weeks preparing all sorts of little surprises and making clothes or toys or pillows for Kathy. Her outlook was beginning to change. Rick was right. Praying together did give them both a new kind of strength. The bright outlook clouded when she thought of Sebrena. She still loathed her. As long as she focused on Kathy coming home she could be cheerful and sunny. But, when she dwelled too long on Sebrena, she felt the bitterness choke her. She and Rick continued to pray about it. She knew it would take time. Finding forgiveness for that woman was unimaginable.

Sebrena clutched her stomach and curled her legs up. She hadn't been this sick since they had taken the Carribean cruise and ran into foul weather. Wynne was right. Kathy must have had the flu and now she was going to suffer through it too. She didn't remember Kathy vomiting though. Maybe she was sick at Julie's and they never told her. Communication was going to have to improve at least while these arrangements were necessary. Meanwhile, what was she going to do? Putting Kathy and Wynne together on their own was a little premature. They needed more time to get used to each other before beginning to cement that father/daughter relationship. Well, there was no choice. She couldn't be vertical for more than a minute without feeling seasick.

"Wynne, sweetheart," Sebrena called through the intercom. "I need you. Can you come up to the bedroom?"

In a few minutes, Wynne entered the room. Sebrena's ghostly pallor alarmed him. It was obvious she was sick and now he'd have to care for Kathy alone. Thank goodness it was Sunday and she was going back to the Sierras.

"Honey," began Sebrena. "I promised Kathy I would take her to church today before she has to go back to the Sierras. I hate to ask you, but I don't want to disappoint her. Could you take her? I've been wanting you to see this church anyway. It would be better if we could go together, but I guess this will have to do."

"I think I can handle that. Why don't I call the Sierras and see if they'll take Kathy a little earlier? That way you can just spend the whole day in bed and not have to worry about her."

"Sounds like a good idea," Sebrena said putting a hand to her forehead. Now she was getting light headed too. She felt so miserable, she would have agreed to most anything.

As usual, Kathy was sitting in the middle of her room playing with her stuffed dogs when Wynne came in. Wynne never saw her put the dogs aside. They were always incorporated into her activities somehow.

"Kathleen, Sebrena is very sick this morning and asked me to take you to church and then to the Sierras today. Can you get ready on your own or do you need me to help?"

"I can do it but you hafta button the back of my dress."

"Sounds like my kind of job. I can handle that."

"Could we go to my reg'lar church today? We're having a special movie in children's church. I'd like to see it."

"You know, that's not a bad idea. Then I could just let the Sierras take you home from church."

"Thanks!" Kathy said with more enthusiasm than he'd heard in a long while.

"Don't mention it," Wynne replied with a wink. "Call me when you need those buttons done."

Wynne phoned Rick Sierra from the den. Just as he thought, the Sierras would be delighted to have Kathy a few hours earlier and were even more excited to know he was bringing her to their church. He purposely neglected to mention the change of churches to Sebrena. There's nothing to be gained in upsetting her, he thought.

When they arrived, Kathy led Wynne by the hand to show him the room that was set up like a little chapel for the children. He shook hands with the adult in charge and patted Kathy on the head as he said good bye. He met Rick in the foyer and told him that he had left Kathy in the children's room.

"Thanks, Wynne. I appreciate you bringing her here. We could have picked her up if Sebrena was sick."

"No, that's all right. Kathy and I had a nice little chat on the way over. She's a cute kid once you get to know her." Wynne looked for the chance to work his way to the door. No sense staying around, he thought. Kathy would be in the other room and never even know he was gone.

"I see you have a visitor," Pastor Simon said to Rick as he extended his hand to Wynne. Rick introduced them without explaining who Wynne was but Pastor Simon recognized the name. He had said it in prayer enough times. "We're glad to have you visit today. I'll look forward to introducing you in our welcome time this morning." Pastor Simon walked away to greet another visitor before Wynne could protest.

Trapped. There was no way Wynne could escape sitting through the service now. Rick began leading Wynne to the sanctuary, greeting people and introducing his visitor along the way.

Julie approached the two then hesitated for a moment realizing it was Wynne who was with her husband. She drew a deep breath and said a quiet, "Help me, Lord." as she started toward them. Smiling, she greeted Wynne and took Rick's hand as an usher led them to a pew.

The music began. As hymnal pages rustled, Julie's mind became frustrated with thoughts of Sebrena and Kathy and Wynne. She fought off the bad feelings. Lowering her head, she prayed silently that God would clear her head and put her heart in tune with worship. She avoided praying for Wynne.

Rick had not avoided prayer for Wynne. He had spent time praying right after Wynne phoned. If Kathy was to have Wynne in her life as a second father, he prayed that God would touch Wynne's heart and turn him to Christ. After all, Rick smiled, God specialized in the impossible.

Wynne began to relax after the welcome time when he had stood with the other visitors while the congregation applauded their welcome. Who could tell, maybe there were some potential votes in the congregation. A little more exposure to the voting public was always beneficial. The church wasn't as bad as he thought it would be. Sebrena's horror stories about Harry didn't seem to apply here. Everyone acted pretty normal and a little religion never hurt. At least it wouldn't give him nightmares.

Michael Boston's camera clicked in rapid succession as he shot frame after frame of Julie and Rick leaving church with Kathy between them. What was it the professor has said in his photography class? If it's worth taking one picture, it's worth five or six more. That gave you a better opportunity to come out with a great shot.

He'd made some promises in order to get the information he needed to confirm his story but he had managed to avoid a "no pictures" commitment. This was going to be one heck of a good feature for a Sunday edition. He decided he wasn't going to peddle it though until he was sure he had everything.

Everything included finding out whether or not Wynne Warner had suddenly got religion. He noticed Wynne leaving the church before the Sierras had appeared. This was not the church Warner claimed membership in. He smiled. Warner's church would probably think him a visitor if he ever showed up there.

Boston set his camera down and pulled away before anyone would notice him. No sense making the subjects overly cautious or shy. He hummed the tune he had heard through his open window being played on the carillon in the church steeple. It seemed oddly familiar. And then he remembered. Someone had sung that at his father's funeral. Something about a rugged cross. He shook the memory before the wave of regret could drown him and drove on.

Fifteen

Pound Puppies

"Mrs. Sierra?"

"Yes," Julie replied, resting the phone between her ear and her shoulder.

"This is Mrs. Katz, Kathy's teacher. I'm sorry to bother you at work, but I think we need to have a talk about Kathy. I was wondering if you would have time to stop in for a few moments when you pick Kathy up from school?"

"Certainly," Julie said with apprehension. "Can you tell me what the problem is?"

"It has to do with Kathy's Pound Puppies and a few other things, but I'd rather we wait until this afternoon when you come. I need to get back to my class in a few minutes."

"Of course. I'll see you later then." Julie replaced the receiver and stood motionless for a moment. In the past, she always enjoyed meeting with Kathy's teachers They all praised her achievement and her behavior. They marveled at her out-going personality and exuberance. She brought an energy to the classroom and a quest for learning that refreshed the weariest teacher. Julie knew today would be different. This was not the same little girl.

The change in Kathy was becoming more obvious to people. She had lost weight and dark circles emphasized her lusterless eyes. Julie took her to Dr. Jansen, and he prescribed some vitamins and more rest. There was nothing wrong physically that he could find to cause the bed wetting and the nightmares or the general listlessness but, then, he didn't know Sebrena. Julie knew she was the cause. Couldn't anyone see what Sebrena was doing to this child?

For a brief moment, Julie considered calling Sebrena about the meeting with Mrs. Katz. Sebrena should be there—legally. Maybe it would sensitize Sebrena and she would release her hold on Kathy. No, Sebrena was not going to give up. Well, she would just assume that Mrs. Katz would call both mothers and hope that Sebrena had been neglected. That would excuse her from any responsibility.

Sebrena wasn't looking too well these days either. Julie wondered sarcastically if motherhood had overwhelmed her. Her crooked smile faded. *Oh, Lord, when will I stop thinking these awful things about her? Will my attitude ever get any better?*

"Pregnant? I can't be pregnant. You said yourself that I couldn't get pregnant because of the damage the abortion had done.'

"No, Mrs. Warner, I said it would be extremely difficult for you to conceive, not impossible." Sebrena's gynecologist tapped his pen on the desk as he spoke.

Sebrena hated the know-it-all attitudes doctors possessed. Erving had been like that too. Sure, he would take care of everything. Nothing to worry about. Well, he hadn't messed things up as badly as she'd thought. Pregnant. How will Wynne take this, she wondered. It had been difficult telling him when they married there would be no family. She felt her worth diminished. She was damaged goods.

"I didn't marry you to become a baby machine," he had said. "Not having babies keeps you free to help me get elected and, as the office gets higher, the elections get harder. A good man needs a beautiful woman at his side to complete the perfect political picture."

Well, at last she would feel like they could complete the picture her way. A good politician should also be a good family man. Wynne could finally have family of his own and Kathy would have a little brother or sister.

Sebrena went straight to Wynne's office after leaving from the doctor's office with a prescription for vitamins and a warning to take life easier. He had warned her to stay off her feet as much as possible. Her ability to carry the child full term concerned him. Marge was away from her desk so Sebrena went straight into Wynne's office.

"Hi, sweetheart. Oops. I'm sorry I thought you were alone," She apologized. She had unintentionally intruded upon Wynne and his campaign manager, Stewart.

"Hi," he replied. "I'll be right with you. We're almost done." He turned back to the papers in his hand and made a few more remarks about fund raising before shaking hands and showing the campaign manager out.

"What brings you here this time of day?" Wynne asked trying not to sound annoyed. His afternoon schedule was already in chaos.

"I wondered if you were free for lunch. Maybe we could find some little nook to eat in together. I have something I'd like to talk to you about." She smiled sweetly.

"I'm sorry. I don't think I'm going to get much more than a coffee and bagel for lunch, and I'm going to have to eat it on the run." Sebrena's eyes watered. Weepy women always did it to him. "Let me buzz Marge and see what's up next. Maybe we can squeeze something in."

"Yes?" Marge answered on Wynne's intercom.

"Marge, how are we doing?"

"I was just going to let you know Sandra James called and canceled her appointment with you, and Stewart said he can't get to the bond proposal yet, so that won't be back for you to review until the morning."

"Thanks. I'm going to take my wife out for a quick lunch. Can you hold the fort?"

"Sure thing. Bon appetit."

"Sebrena," he said, "It's going to have to be fast. I'm still playing catch up this afternoon. How about Lorenzo's Deli?"

"I suppose that will have to do." Sebrena was disappointed. She had wanted a cozy nook somewhere special to tell him her news. Lorenzo's was fast, crowded and noisy.

Wynne questioned her all the way to the deli. She was a little girl with a secret, bursting with anticipation of revelation but enjoying the power of privileged knowledge.

Her coy smile wavered however when she noticed the odd couple sitting across the room at the window and looking in their direction.

Ray and Judge Helen were looking at the Warners. "Isn't that one of the couples in that difficult case we had a few weeks ago?" Ray asked Helen. He took another bite of his pastrami on rye.

"Yup. That's Wynne Warner and his wife. I'm curious to know how things are going," replied Helen."Aren't they about due to sign the final papers for the agreement?"

"I think it's on the docket in a couple of weeks."

"I sure hope everything works out for that little girl. I've been praying for her." Helen cut another piece of stromboli and fussed with the string of mozzarella cheese that wouldn't let go of the rest of the sandwich.

"You really like that stuff, don't you." Ray said.

"Yeah. I should be eating a salad though but I really like the cheese."

"That's not what I meant."

"Oh. What did you mean?"

"I meant praying. You do a lot of that now. What made you so religious all of a sudden?"

"You did." Helen smiled at his obvious bewilderment.

"I did?"

"Uh huh. You're the one who told me I needed the wisdom of Solomon. The only way I know to get that is to read my Bible and pray. It's paid off too. I feel a lot more confident in my decisions now. At least I know I'm open to God's leading, and since He knows a lot more about these people who come through my court than I do, I figure He's tho one who ought to be making the judgements."

"Sounds heavy."

"Have you ever known a court of law where things didn't get heavy? Even Judge Judy has her troublesome days."

Ray smiled and shook his head. Helen was a unique lady.

"You know, Ray, I've even been praying for you. You're very important to me, not only as a law clerk, but as a friend as well."

"Ordinarily, I'd protest. But the way you talk about prayer, and mean it, I kind of like the idea of you praying for me. Who knows what might happen?"

"God knows. Someday, Ray, when you're ready to listen, there's something I'd like to tell you about. It could change your life."

Ray smiled at her again. She knew he wasn't ready yet. He knew it too. But, he was coming very close to asking her just what made her Jesus so important to her.

Their attention was drawn to the commotion at the Warner's table. Warner was standing with his hand roughly grasping the arm of a man with a camera. The whole crowd in the deli heard him say something about what the man could do with his camera and his newspaper. As the man turned to leave, Helen and Ray noticed a big grin spreading the breadth of his face. Unusual for a man who had just been insulted. Warner was throwing money on the table, obviously in a hurry to leave.

"Well, hello," Ray drawled. "A little free entertainment. I wonder what that was all about?"

"Hopefully nothing that has anything to do with our business," Helen replied savoring the last bite of her stromboli and wondering if she should pop a Tums now or when she got back to the courthouse.

"She's been missing a lot of what is going on in class," Mrs. Katz continued after sending Kathy to the other end of the room to play. "The daydreaming is not what bothers me the most. It's her Pound Puppies. They have been coming to school regularly now and she seems to have a desperate attachment to them. Mrs. Warner made her leave them at home one day and she cried almost the entire day."

Julie observed Kathy across the room in animated conversation with Wilbur and Barnaby. Yes, she noticed the Pound Puppies becoming more important to Kathy but she hadn't considered it detrimental.

"Kathy has cut herself off from the other children during recess. She takes the puppies to the wall of the building, sits alone and talks to them. She rarely responds in class, and I know she's not getting her homework done. I'm very concerned. Perhaps you might consider getting Kathy some professional help to get her through this difficult period."

"Have you mentioned this to Mrs. Warner?"

"Not exactly. Well not all of it," Mrs. Katz replied. "Mrs. Warner thought I was only complaining about the puppies. She never gave me a chance to explain everything."

"I'm sorry. This is a difficult time for all of us. The court decision has put you in a bad spot too."

"It's not your fault, Mrs. Sierra. If I didn't care about Kathy so much, I'm not sure how I would cope with the confusion either. If this is so difficult for all of us as adults, think of what it must be like for her. Her life is divided in two."

Julie hung her head. Her face reddened and swelled with the onset of tears. Every time she thought things might get better, that they might be able to work this out, a new crisis would present itself. Mrs. Katz was right. They were tearing Kathy in two.

"And, Mrs. Sierra, there's one more thing." Mrs. Katz laid a comforting hand on Julie's arm and leaned forward. "When Kathy is at your home, she wants us to call her 'Kathy'. But, when she is at the Warner's home, she wants to be called 'Kathleen'. It's as though she's becoming two different personalities. Please think about therapy. It would help you all to cope better."

"I'll discuss it with my husband and we'll talk it over with the Warners," Julie said rising to leave. "Thank you, Mrs. Katz. I deeply appreciate your love and concern for Kathy."

Mrs. Katz nodded. Julie could see the tears brimming in her eyes too. *Why God? Why are You doing this?* She asked the same question over and over as she drove home.

Julie related Mrs. Katz's concerns to Rick after dinner while Kathy was occupied in her room. They decided to face the Warners with the problem and try to arrange some professional help for all of them.

"After all, there's enough of us to make it group therapy," Rick quipped. "Seriously, there has to be a way for all of us to deal with this situation."

"The thought of discussing this with Sebrena makes my skin crawl," Julie replied.

"Let's pray about it," Rick said taking her hand in his . Together they asked for God's direction.

Julie finished the dishes and climbed the stairs to check on Kathy. Kathy was so involved with Wilbur and Barnaby that she didn't notice Julie standing in the doorway. A shiver went down Julie's spine as she began to understand what Kathy was saying to the puppies.

"We have to be careful that Kathleen doesn't play in this room anymore. She's a bad girl when she visits here. Wilbur, you have to help me keep her out of the closet. Mommy is going to be mad if she sees the clothes. She may send me away forever."

"Well, Barnaby," Kathy continued in a little different tone, "I don't know that I want Kathy to come and live with us forever at Sebrena's. She cries all the time and makes Sebrena mad when she wets the bed. I don't like her."

Tears fell down Julie's cheeks as she eavesdropped on the conversation between her daughter and her precious puppies. Was this a little girl's fantasy play, or did she really believe she was two different people?

As Kathy stood, she made one final remark to the two polyester-stuffed friends that cut through Julie's heart. "Maybe it would be better if I would just die." Kathy shrugged her shoulders and picked up the puppies. She almost dropped them when Julie startled her by entering the room. Color drained from her face and she stood frozen to the spot.

Julie carefully approached her precious child and wrapped her arms around her gently. "Kathy, I love you so much. I wish you never had to go back to the Warners' and everything could be like it was." It took all the self control Julie had to keep from falling apart at that moment.

Kathy stood rigid as a wooden soldier. When Julie looked into her eyes, they looked vacant. Kathy didn't seem to be listening. She was deliberately shutting Julie out. It was too painful to love. No one really wanted her anyway, Kathy thought, just Wilbur and Barnaby.

Julie remembered Kathy's remark about the clothes. Opening the closet door, she found all the items hung on hangers had been marked with a large X in black ink. It was a crushing blow. Julie managed to tell Kathy it was bedtime and escaped quickly. Alone in her room, Julie's heart cried out to God. *Lord what do you want from me? Haven't we paid enough for my misjudgement? Why are you taking it out on Kathy? Me. I'm the one who was wrong. It should be me you're punishing not Kathy. Her life shouldn't be sacrificed for my mistake.*

She waited a moment, as if expecting God to audibly answer her. Her answer came in remembering Abraham and Isaac. God had asked Abraham to sacrifice Isaac, his only son and foreseeable answer to God's promise of building a nation through Abraham. Abraham had almost plunged the knife into Isaac when God spoke and provided another sacrifice.

Julie lay quietly on the bed. Jesus, God's only son, had been the greatest sacrifice. He had died for her mistakes, her sins. The price had already been paid. God was not making Kathy pay for them again. Kathy was suffering for Julie's mistake, but she knew in her heart that God would provide a way out, just as He had provided the ram in the bushes for Abraham. She just had to look for it. But where?

The answer came quietly. . .within.

Sixteen
Headlines

The newspaper hit the table with a thud in front of Sebrena. She jumped, spilling coffee over the placemat.

"What!?" was all she could manage to recover of speech from the surprise and then the realization that her angry face was staring up at her from the front page. There, beside her at the table in the deli, Wynne looked just as angry. Next to their unflattering photo was a picture of Julie and Rick walking with Kathy between them coming out of the church door. The bold printed headline "FATHER TO BE?" was underscored by a smaller one that read, "Aborted Child Object of Custody Battle".

Sebrena's gasp escaped through the hand she'd placed over her mouth. She looked up at Wynne who was pacing. Every muscle in his face twitched. A vein pulsed in his neck. The phone rang and she rose to answer it.

"No," Wynne ordered. "I'd better handle the phone." He picked it up with a brusk, "Hello." His red face deepened in color. " No comment. No, there will be no interviews on this subject. When I'm ready to give my stand on abortion, I'll call you." He banged the phone down but it immediately rang again. Over and over Wynne gave the same answers to call after call. Each one challenged him to choose a side in the abortion issue. Finally, he took the phone off the hook and placed it in the kitchen drawer.

"This is the nightmare I feared," he said looking at Sebrena. His anger and pain revealed in his face. "Thanks to you, my political career is going down the tubes in a hurry."

"No, Honey, I can't believe that," Sebrena retorted. "This is just another opportunity to show people what a wonderful state senator you would make. Everyone knows abortion is a woman's right. By supporting me through this custody ordeal, they will know where you stand and respect you for it."

"You don't understand, Sebrena. I'm not sure myself where I stand on abortion. I've always felt it was O.K. in extreme cases where a mother's life is threatened, or rape or incest occurred, or there were other extenuating medical circumstances, but not just as a means of birth control or family planning. My involvement with Kathy's custody is because you're my wife. It doesn't have anything to do with my sanctioning your actions before we were married. I've avoided thinking about that. I was afraid it might change my feelings for you. I have a hard time condoning your reasons for the attempted abortion. Kathy is a beautiful child. If you'd had your way, she wouldn't be here now." He shook his head.

"God help me, maybe that would have been easier for all of us." Wynne grabbed his briefcase before she could respond and stormed out the door.

Sebrena sat down and unfolded the paper so she could begin reading the story. She had to retrace the beginning sentences a few times until Wynne's words finally stopped echoing in her head. The story presented both sides and supplied a good deal of information that Sebrena thought confidential. Her mind began to click out the possibilities of turning this to her advantage. Surely the reporter needed to know the illegalities of how the Sierras obtained

Kathy. They were only hinted at. If she gave him the hard facts he could present them for the criminals they were rather than letting them look like the goodie two shoed rescuers some people would proclaim them to be.

Retrieving the phone from the drawer she hung it on its hook again. Just as she turned away, it rang. "Hello?" she said trying to be pleasant. After all, she was the future senator's wife and it was her job to be pleasant and supportive.

"Is this Sebrena Warner?" The voice sounded strange.

"Yes, yes it is."

"Murderer! Baby Killer! You should be cut into pieces slowly just like you wanted to do to that poor baby!"

"I. . ." she started, but didn't get the chance to finish before the line clicked and went dead. She hung up the phone and began molding her plan.

Rick sat in stunned silence while Julie rose to collect another tissue from the box on the counter. She dabbed at her red nose. The newspaper lay spread out on the kitchen table where the two had read with sickening interest Michael Boston's story. It centered more on Wynne and Sebrena throwing innuendo out to create a stir over his intent to run for state office in the spring primaries. The paper showed a picture of the birth certificate made out as baby "Jane Doe" and signed by Dr. Erving. The reporter could not get Dr. Erving to cooperate but he indicated the hospital would be doing its own investigation. It went on to say that there were a lot of questions yet to be answered about the legality of the adoption. Julie hadn't expected him to print that.

Rick looked at her again. His eyes searing through her. "How in the world could you have told him without even a hint to me of what you were doing? Why, Julie, why?"

"I truly thought it would help. If Wynne were confronted with publicity, I thought he might get Sebrena to back off. I didn't know he would dig so deep and involve us so much in the story. He told me he was more interested in whether or not this would force Wynne to take some kind of political stand on abortion. He just needed confirmation that Sebrena had tried to abort Kathy. He told me he would keep his source confidential."

"He's a journalist, Julie, a news reporter. He's going to dig and dig until he can come up with the best selling story he can get. He's in the business to sell stories not to help with custody cases. I can't believe you did this. I can't believe you could be this stupid."

"I. . .I'm sorry." Julie could barely get the words out. She wasn't even sure he'd heard her as he went out the door. Rick had never been this angry with her. She had never felt so disappointed in herself. Fear and panic were taking over. What would Rick do? Would they be in more trouble now if Boston dug up more facts? Her only wish at the moment was to crawl back under the covers of the bed and sleep until everything was over. She didn't want to have to think any more. She couldn't deal with Rick's anger. She felt dejected, defeated, alone. What promise did tomorrow hold?

"Tomorrow had better bring some sound hard facts in here," Bart barked as he shuffled stacks of folders and papers on his desk. "You don't have any lime light to bask in until you get those facts lined up and confirmed. I took a chance printing that story with just your anonymous source to back you up. Now, you'd better get your act together."

"Sure, Bart. O.K. Tomorrow." Boston grinned. If he could convince one side to talk, he could probably break down the other side. Then he could get those juicy little facts Bart wanted about how the Sierras managed an adoption without consent of the mother or an agency. There was a lawyer involved here too. That would be great. People always loved reading about lawyers getting their due. Warner's wife would spill. He felt it in his gut. He just needed to get her off somewhere, alone, without her husband.

"Haul out of here, Boston," Bart ordered making him jump as his concentration was broken.

"Hey, I'm history."

"Get the rest of the story or you really will be."

Michael moved through the maze of activity and confusion called a newspaper office and found his desk just as he'd left it. Piled to the hilt with faxes and computer printouts from his research into the custody case. He reached for his phone knocking over a styrofoam cup of old coffee. A few choice words flew into the air, annoying the religious editor that sat two desks away. Frantically he dabbed with whatever napkins he could find in his trash can. Preliminary damage covered, he took off for the cubby hole where they kept the coffee pot and paper towels. He was too far away to hear his phone ringing.

Sebrena heard the mechanical voice mail tell her to give her message. Hesitantly, she said, "This is Sebrena Warner. I need to talk to you about your story but I don't want to do it over the phone. Please meet me at Brielle's coffee shop in Independence at two."

Brielle's was away from downtown bustle and had New York style high backed booths that would give them some privacy.

She went to her closet to decide what would best fit the situation. Nothing too flashy, or too businesslike, it had to be something that would make her look soft and vulnerable. A mother image but yet holding forth that she was an intelligent woman, one to be taken seriously. She tried five different combinations before she finally found one that suited her. It was a dark teal dress with a dainty floral pattern, simple lines but not tailored. It had a scooped neck that would show off her single strand of pearls. She let her hair fall around her face and was careful to keep her makeup light. She was pleased with the final inspection in the full length mirror.

"Rick Sierra. How can I help you?" Rick caught a glimpse of his face in the mirrored collage that decorated the wall opposite his desk. His face clearly showed that the morning was not going well. He wouldn't be surprised to find himself cleaning out his desk by the end of it. The heads of the pharmaceutical company were not pleased with the information in the paper this morning and word had come down through his boss that any more bad publicity, especially with the mention of where he worked, would not bode well for his future with the company. He was almost relieved to hear Wynne's voice.

"Rick, have you seen the paper?"

"Unfortunately I have as well as a score of other people around here."

"We need to talk. Neither one of us needs this kind of publicity and I'm afraid that little girl is going to suffer as well. How's your schedule? Can we get together this morning, say 9:30?"

"My schedule may be more open than I care for soon. Nine thirty would be fine. Where shall we meet?"

Wynne suggested a hotel restaurant before hanging up and leaving Rick to his thoughts again. Well, maybe Julie was right. Maybe this will change Wynne's direction, and he will influence Sebrena. And maybe the sun will be blue tomorrow. Wynne would probably look for them to give in. The hole just seemed to get deeper, and he felt like he was going to be swallowed up and buried.

Wynne had been right, Rick thought as he headed for the table in the back of the hotel restaurant. This was a quiet place to meet. The breakfast crowd had left and it was too early for lunch to be served. As Rick approached, Wynne rose and extended his hand. Even though Rick had prayed a great deal with Pastor Simon anticipating a meeting like this, he still felt apprehensive and ill at ease.

The waitress took their orders for coffee and sweet rolls and left the men to their business meeting. Rick and Wynne let out a long low sigh simultaneously. Surprised, they looked at each other and broke out in smiles. Their common reflex had broken the ice.

"I don't know where to begin this," Rick said. "Not only do we have to deal with this publicity, but I feel that, as fathers, we need to talk about what is happening to Kathy. Some kind of consistency has to be established between our homes that will help her to adjust to living with both of us."

"I know what you mean," Wynne said nodding a thank you to the waitress as she poured steaming coffee into their cups.

"Have you noticed how she's changed? She's always tired and seems to be losing weight. And those dark circles are always there under her eyes no matter how much sleep she gets." Rick paused to sip his coffee.

"Yes, I've noticed. She isn't the same little girl Sebrena first brought to our home. By the way, I've meant to apologize for that for some time now. I didn't know what she was planning. I certainly wouldn't have condoned it."

"I can understand that. Sebrena seems to be a very impulsive woman. Maybe that's what's gotten us all into this situation—all of us being too impulsive."

"How can I help, Rick? I'm newer at this fathering experience than you are. And I want to help Kathy. She's a spunky kid. Got a lot of courage."

"Maybe we could try to give her a little more common ground. Going to the same school helps. Do you think attending the same church would lend a little more stability too? Julie and I would be willing to compromise and find a church that we could all agree on just so Kathy could have more consistency." Secretly, Rick prayed that Wynne would suggest that Kathy stay at her present church.

"I appreciate what you're trying to do, Rick. Sebrena and I have never been much for church going. Kathy talked Sebrena into it a few times, but I know, because of her first husband, it's hard for Sebrena to go. I wouldn't be opposed to just leaving Kathy with the church group she's accustomed to now. I must admit, I kind of enjoyed your church service that day. Maybe I can talk Sebrena into it. At the very least, I could be sure that Kathy makes it to Sunday school and church each week."

"Thanks," Rick replied. A sigh of relief escaped. "I was hoping you might say that. There are a lot of loving and caring people in that church and I know they will help us all through this transition time until Kathy learns to accept that she has two sets of parents. With God's help, we will all survive this turmoil."

Wynne drew a deep breath. "What do you know about Michael Boston from the News Herald?"

"Not much. He came to our door the day we went over to get Kathy from you. He wanted to run a missing person story. I felt he was expecting more. And, he was too agreeable when I asked him not to write anything. He left me with a very uneasy feeling. I guess he was saving himself for a bigger story." Rick failed to mention Julie's involvement in giving Boston information. He didn't want to make Wynne angry when things were going so well.

"He's going to dog us until he gets the story he's looking for." Wynne noticed that Rick was averting his eyes. "We have to all agree that we will not give him anything to feed on. I can't stand any more publicity about Sebrena's abortion, and I'm sure you don't need to have anything exposed about Kathy's adoption. Our feelings aside, Kathy doesn't need to be made to feel like a freak because of the circumstances of her birth with media hounding her. Hopefully our town is a small enough potato that the story won't go any farther. I don't want her to be the object of a feeding frenzy for the press."

"Agreed." Rick said meeting Wynne's gaze again. He was beginning to like this man in spite of himself.

Wynne and Rick went on to exchange information about themselves. People observing them saw two men discussing their careers as though the were old friends catching up on some missing years.

Wynne left with more questions than ever about Rick. He's been through so much for Kathy. How does he keep on going? And, the way he spoke about God, it was as if he knew Him as a personal friend. How could a man speak so easily and comfortably about his faith? Wynne knew he wouldn't be so gracious or so forgiving if he had been in Rick's shoes. What was it that made him so different?

Rick parted with a good feeling about Wynne. He wasn't a bad character after all. Rick turned the old blue Chevy onto the freeway. Everything went well, he thought. Wynne appeared genuinely concerned for Kathy. He could share Kathy's affections much better knowing that Wynne truly cared for her well being too.

Rick hit the brake pedal as the truck in front of him began to slow. The car was slowing but a sudden screech accompanied by a jolt from behind propelled him into the back of the truck. With little time to react, he covered his face and ducked.

Seventeen

Conviction

Thankfully the coffee shop was not busy when Sebrena arrived. She took a seat in the back booth sitting all the way to the edge of the seat so that she could see around the tall backrest, and watch for Michael Boston to enter. Ordering a latte, she nervously played with the blue packages of sweetener on the table, keeping her eyes peeled to the door.

Shortly after 2:30, Boston strode confidently through the door. He paused a moment to let his eyes adjust to the dimmer light. Sebrena waved slightly and he followed the waitress to the back booth as she delivered Sebrena's latte.

"What can I get for you?" the waitress asked as he took a seat across from Sebrena.

"Just a house brew, black. Thanks." Michael didn't care for all the flavored coffees. He felt he'd have to drink them with his pinky sticking out. Coffee was coffee and black was best. Don't mess with it. It only took a moment for the waitress to return with his order.

"Well," Michael started, "Where do you want to begin?"

"I read your story this morning. It's really very slanted against Wynne and me."

"I had to use the facts that I had and what was substantiated through my source. Do you care to enlighten me further?"

"I think you need to be fair and present the facts about the false adoption. Julie and Rick managed to adopt Kathy with no consent from me or any agency. Since I didn't know Kathy had survived, I couldn't give consent. And, since Dr. Erving did not want his incompetence made public, he didn't refer the baby to an agency. He just let Julie handle it all."

"Do you realize that Dr. Erving denies all this?"

"I'm sure he does. He's facing dismissal from the hospital and having his license investigated. And, if Wynne and I decide to pursue this further, we could bring malpractice charges against him. Of course he would deny it."

"So how do I know that the Sierras faked the adoption?"

"Here is a copy of Kathy's adoption papers." Sebrena pulled some papers from her purse. "Our lawyer was able to obtain them because of the circumstances of the case. You'll notice that the one giving consent is signed 'Sharon Smith'. How that notary could accept that name is a mystery, unless she was in on it somehow. I'm sure Sharon Smith would turn out to fit Julie's description."

Michael looked at the copies. He tried to contain the excitement building inside. This was it. Just what he needed.

"Mr. Boston, at the time Kathy was born, I was in a very difficult situation. I may have made some wrong choices, but we do what we have to do at the time. I am not the horrible person some people would like to think." She rubbed her arms as if cold, remembering the words shouted at her that morning on the phone.

"Is Kathy Wynne's daughter?"

"I think I've given you all the information you need to balance the story, Mr. Boston. I do need to run. I have an appointment that I'm already late for." Sebrena rose and gathered her purse. Michael started to reach his hand out to her but she moved away and headed for the door.

"That'll be six dollars." Michael turned his head to see the waitress laying the check on the table. Six dollars. Well, that was probably the least he'd ever had to pay for information before.

Julie stepped out of the delivery room wiping a tear from her eye. The couple who had just delivered a healthy little girl made her ache for Rick. She wondered what it would have been like to have Rick standing next to her, holding her hand and coaching her breathing while she delivered their child. He would have been a great birthing coach. His strength and encouragement was what kept her going. Now, she despaired over the disappointment she had brought him with this morning's news story. Why did she keep doing the things she did? She felt like she was spiraling downward, losing everything along the way.

"Julie, there's a call for you." Carrie's voice startled Julie out of her daydream. Carrie stared at her in a strange way as she took the phone.

"This is Julie Sierra," she said and then the world seemed to stop.

"Julie, there's been an accident," the emergency room nurse told her as gently as she could. "Rick was involved. The paramedics are bringing him in by ambulance."

"No, oh God, no. I'll be right down." She could feel Carrie's hands lending her support.

"I'm coming with you," Carrie said as another nurse appeared to cover the desk. Together they ran down the stairs to the emergency room.

Rick was just arriving. As the gurney passed Julie, her hands flew to her mouth to suppress a scream. Her professional training was forgotten. This was Rick. Her love. Her life. How badly was he hurt? *Oh, God, the blood. Please, don't let him die.*

Julie collapsed into the chair where Carrie led her. Someone brought a cool compress for her head.

"Julie, honey, I know it's your husband, but think. Think, Julie. You know they always look worse than they are when they first get here. It may not be that bad. Calm down, breathe slowly, and then we can go check on his injuries." Carrie was brushing strands of hair from Julie's face.

Looking inside for the strength she needed, Julie finally nodded to Carrie and they went into the examining room. Activity bustled around Rick. Julie made her way through the maze of people and took Rick's hand in hers.

"Rick, I'm here, sweetheart. I love you. Hang on, Rick."

"Julie, you'll have to leave," Dr. Evans said quietly. "We have some work to do here. I'll get to you as soon as we know anything. Please trust me."

The echo of the heart monitor rang in Julie's ears as she left the room. In a daze, she mechanically made the turns in the corridors that led her to the little chapel. She sat in the last pew. Dry eyed, she stared straight ahead at the multicolored glass behind the cross. *Prayer? I can't, Lord. I'm all prayed out.*

Wynne walked into the kitchen expecting to see the table set as usual when he came in from work. He could smell dinner. It had the aroma of home cooking. A glance in the dining room revealed preparations for a special evening. Good china, silver and crystal graced the three lace place mats. Tulips, iris and little yellow asters filled a bowl that sat between silver candlesticks aglow with candles.

"Did I forget something? Are we having company for dinner?" he asked Sebrena as she placed individual salad plates full of spinach, mandarin oranges and bacon bits next to the dinner plates.

"Just a captivating evening for my two most favorite people," Sebrena chimed as she smiled at Kathy and then Wynne.

"Well that aroma has certainly captivated me. Let's eat." Wynne felt his spirits lift at the anticipation of a great meal. Among many other redeeming attributes, Sebrena was a good cook.

Wynne suspected more than just dessert would finish this meal. Sebrena had been keeping something from him ever since their lunch at Lorenzo's when Boston had interrupted them. Sebrena rarely went all out like this for just the two, or rather now the three of them. What was she up to?

"I wanted to make tonight memorable for us," Sebrena said as they were finishing up the last bites of a chocolate mousse torte. "I have something very important to tell the two of you." Sebrena paused until she had their attention. "We're going to have a baby."

There was a moment of silence as her statement hung in the air. Kathy broke it by saying, " That's nice." Then she went back to pushing pieces of her torte back and forth on the plate.

Wynne was still stunned. A baby?

"Well, what do you think? Are you ready to become a father again?" Sebrena's lip was quivering. The scene that was played out in her mind earlier was Wynne jumping up and running to her to embrace her with joy. He was just sitting there, mouth slightly ajar.

"Well? Are you ready to become a father again?" Sebrena repeated.

"I. . .I didn't. . .I wasn't. . .I am? We are?"

"Well, well, a politician at a loss for words." Sebrena reached for her glass of water. "A toast. To you, Dad." Before she could raise the glass to her lips, the phone rang. Wynne rushed to answer it, grateful for the opportunity to think for a few minutes away from Sebrena.

Wynne's hand tightened on the receiver as the story Julie was telling him began to take hold. Wynne felt a wave of regret go through him. Rick. How could this happen to Rick. He's such a good person.

"I need to talk to Kathy, Wynne," Julie said. "I don't want her to hear it on the news."

"Would you like me to tell her? I can imagine how difficult this must be for you."

"No, I want to tell her. She doesn't trust me like she used to, and I don't want to lose what little trust may be left by not sharing the truth with her. I would appreciate any help you can give by talking to her when I'm done."

"Sure, Julie. I'm really sorry. I like Rick. We got to know each other a lot better this morning. Please, let me help any way I can."

"Thanks."

Wynne fetched Kathy and watched as Kathy heard the news about Rick's accident. A large tear formed and rolled down her cheek. She nodded her head and gave the phone back to Wynne.

"Julie?" Wynne could hear her sobbing. "Julie, I'll look after Kathy. You take care of yourself and tell Rick I'm pulling for him." She mumbled something before she hung up leaving Wynne with a hollow feeling inside. Rick would pull through. He had to. Wynne hugged Kathy and promised her that Rick would be all right. "We'll go to the hospital in the morning and you can see him and Mommy too."

Wynne didn't notice the pout on Sebrena's face. Here was Julie interfering in her life again, she thought. Would she ever be rid of that woman?

Julie took a deep breath when she hung up the phone. She still felt shaky but she wasn't going to take the Valium Carrie offered. She needed to be there for Rick. Tonight would be critical.

Rick was so still. There was no flicker of life visible. Julie sat in the chair beside his bed. She took his hand in hers and stroked it lightly as she watched his face for any sign of response. The angry words from the morning came back to haunt her. They hadn't even kissed good bye. She bit her lower lip and closed the upper one tightly.

God. Father, what have I done? I don't know where to begin. Forgive me. I've been selfish and self-serving. I've shut You out more than I've asked You in. I haven't trusted You to take care of things. I realize I can't do anything on my own and certainly You are the only one in control of Rick's life. I give him all to You, Lord. If it means I lose him, at least I will know he is with You. Not mine, but Your will be done.

For a moment, Julie thought she had felt a slight twitch in Rick's hand. She couldn't be sure. Gently, she laid her head down on the bed, her face touching his hand. She felt a peace begin to fall on her.

Kathy looked pitiful and insignificant in the huge hospital corridors. She grasped Wynne's hand tightly. They met Julie in the lounge on the floor where Rick's room was. Her face evidenced a sleepless night.

"Hi, Kathy," she said lifting her daughter up and hugging her tightly. "Daddy is doing better this morning. And, I think you can take a peek at him if you want to."

Kathy nodded her head. She was obviously confused and frightened. Julie thanked Wynne and then led Kathy to Rick's room. Heavy drapes blocked the morning sun leaving the room with a dark gloomy feeling. Rick lay very still on the bed. Bandages concealed most of his face and a green plastic tube ran out from his nose. There was another tube that connected his arm to a bag of something that looked like water to Kathy and hung on a big metal pole next to the bed. A funny beeping sound came from a metal box with squiggly lines running across it.

Kathy touched Rick's hand. It didn't close on hers like it usually did and it felt cold. Very cold. Kathy turned and ran from the room colliding with Wynne who stood waiting in the corridor. He caught her in his arms, sweeping her up and holding her shaky body tightly against his.

"What's the matter, little one?"

"Daddy's dead. He's dead. And. . .and it's all my fault. I've been bad." She began to cry.

"Daddy's not dead, Kathy," Julie said trying to get Kathy to look at her. Kathy kept burying her head in Wynne's chest. "Daddy's just sleeping. He fought very hard last night to get better for us. He's very tired and he needs to rest so he'll be able to heal. Come on Honey, let's go down to the cafeteria and get Mommy some breakfast and you some hot chocolate. Maybe, when we come back, Daddy will wake up."

Wynne set Kathy down. She looked up at him, face blotched with red and wet with tears. Kneeling next to her, he took out his hanky and daubed at the wet spots. A strange feeling overtook him. So, this is love, Wynne thought. When did it happen? When did my heart open to let this little one in?

"Julie," Wynne said standing again. "I'd like to go in and see Rick for a few minutes if you don't mind."

"I guess," Julie replied hesitantly. "Rick would probably appreciate your concern."

Wynne braced himself as he headed for Rick's room. He didn't like hospitals. The smell of medicine, disinfectant and misery seemed to permeate the halls. He knew this was a place for healing but in his experience it had never offered that.

He quietly pulled a chair up to the bed. As he looked at Rick, he recalled their conversation the previous morning. The thought occurred to him that, if he could have had a brother, he wished it would have been someone like Rick.

"God," Wynne whispered feeling self-conscious. *"I haven't talked with You much in the past. Guess I shouldn't expect you to listen now, but this man here seems to believe You can do anything. For his sake, I'd like to ask You to help. He's a good man, God. He loves You with all his heart. I could see that yesterday. Help him, please."*

Wynne looked up for a moment. He noticed a slight movement in Rick's eyelids. With fascination he watched Rick try to open his eyes.

"Mmm I doin'?" Rick said groggily. "Gonna die?. . . Not 'fraid."

Wynne grasped Rick's hand quickly. "No, Rick, you're O.K. Take it easy. Doctors say you're gonna be fine." Wynne stopped as he realized Rick was deeply asleep again. He sat with Rick's hand clasped in his.

Julie left Kathy and her hot chocolate at one of the tables in the cafeteria with the admonition to stay put while Mommy got her breakfast. She didn't notice Michael Boston walking toward the table as she moved toward the serving line.

Michael sat down across from Kathy. "Hi, Kathy. I'm a friend of your Daddy. How is he?"

Kathy looked at him. As tears brimmed over again she said, "Daddy's dead."

Michael was stunned. "I thought he was doing better." He watched Kathy fight to control her emotions.

"Mommy said he was better. But I saw him. I know he's dead. I killed him."

"No you didn't. He was in an accident," Michael replied tenderly. This was beginning to bring back memories he didn't want to deal with. He was only twelve when his father died, and he'd blamed himself. If he hadn't been out foolishly racing his horse over the countryside in the bad weather, his father would not have been out in the old pickup that hydroplaned off the curve in the road just above the creek. If the rain hadn't swelled the creek, he might have survived. If. If. If. If only he hadn't been so head strong, demanding his way. He'd struggled with those ifs all his life

"No, I made him die," Kathy argued. "I was mean when he made me stay with Sebrena." Kathy started sobbing.

"What are you doing here?!" Julie demanded reaching the table as quickly as possible after spotting Boston with her daughter. "Haven't you caused enough pain all ready?"

"Look, you didn't have to give me that information for the story," he said defensively. "I didn't twist your arm."

"A decision I will regret the rest of my life."

"Kathy says Rick died. I thought he was doing better."

"He is. He was sleeping when Kathy was in. You can see that Kathy is easily upset. She doesn't know who to believe or trust anymore. And, you hounding her isn't going to make the situation better. Now she has Rick's accident to deal with as well as this crazy custody thing. Have some compassion."

Michael looked at Kathy sitting in the big chair, her hot chocolate untouched before her, head bowed. The news reporter fought with the twelve year old inside who agonized with Kathy. He rose awkwardly.

"Sorry to have bothered you," Michael half whispered. "Glad he's doing better." He walked briskly out of the cafeteria.

Pastor Simon was in the lounge with Julie and Kathy when Wynne returned from Rick's room. Kathy was cuddled in Julie's lap. Both were sound asleep.

"How is he?" Pastor Simon asked.

"He woke up for a moment. Maybe he's starting to come around."

"How about a cup of coffee downstairs? You look like you could use one."

"Sounds good." Wynne figured his office schedule could wait a little longer.

He wouldn't be much good right now anyway. He needed to talk to someone and he knew Pastor Simon and Rick were close friends.

"You know, when Rick woke up for that moment, he said something that keeps running through my head." The pastor and Wynne found a table near the window with a view of the courtyard. "Rick asked me if he was going to die, and then he said he wasn't afraid. He certainly is a strong individual."

"That's true, but Rick's inner strength comes from a special source. I can tell you why he's not afraid to die."

"I think I'm beginning to understand, but tell me more. Tell me what Rick believes."

Pastor Simon told Wynne about a loving God who gave up his only son for Rick and for Wynne and for anyone else who would open his heart to Him and love Him as Lord and Savior. "But, He is more than just Lord, He is your friend. One that is closer than a brother."

Julie's eyes fluttered open. She looked down at the peaceful face nestled in her lap. Gently she brushed the hair back from Kathy's face. A strange calm was beginning to take over her. She had berated herself all night. Her family was hurting and it was all her fault. She was going to have to do what she knew God truly wanted her to do. To give them to Him. She had given Rick to God last night. In the darkest hour, she had let everything rest in His hands. God gave Rick back to her but not before she realized that she had to give Kathy to Him too—completely, with no reservation. She prayed for the courage to follow through.

Eighteen

Decisions

Three weeks had passed quickly. Rick longed to be back at work just to feel useful again. The ribs were healing but he still felt like he'd been hit by a truck. Oh, that's right, he thought, I was. He smiled sardonically. The headaches had finally disappeared, and he could stand without feeling nauseous. The first two weeks home from the hospital passed pleasantly with his two nurses, Julie and Kathy, fawning over him, but now it was doubly lonely since Julie returned to work and Kathy went back to the Warners.

Thanksgiving had been significant for two reasons this year. They had Rick's healing to be thankful for and it was the first holiday they spent without Kathy. It was probably just as well she spent it with the Warners since he and Julie had eaten their turkey off of hospital trays in his room.

Rick reflected on the information Julie had related to him of her meeting with Mrs. Katz just before his accident. Kathy appeared more cheerful when he first came home from the hospital, but as the week wore on, he observed her regression to self absorption and moodiness. When it came time to leave for the Warner's, she was sullen, clutching Barnaby and Wilbur as she followed Sebrena to the car. Certainly therapy was needed, Rick agreed, as much for us as for Kathy. That was most likely what Julie wanted to discuss tonight.

"Mr. Warner, this is Mrs. Katz, Kathy's teacher." Wynne wondered why she was calling him. If Kathy were ill, Sebrena should be notified. "I'm sorry to have to make this phone call, but we have a problem with Kathy. She's suddenly become uncontrollable. She starting throwing books and games and jars of paint. It took all my strength to stop her and get her out of the room so no one would get hurt. I'm sorry, but someone will have to come and get her. She screamed at me when I suggested calling Mrs. Warner and then she said I could call you. Can you come and get her?"

Wynne was stunned. What should he do? He had appointments all afternoon. But, his heart melted thinking of poor Kathy acting out her frustration the only way she knew how. "Yes, Mrs. Katz. It may take me a half hour to get there. I have to get my secretary to make a few schedule changes, then I'll be on my way."

"Oh, thank you." The relief was evident in Mrs. Katz's voice.

In his car, Wynne pondered the reasons Kathy wanted him instead of Sebrena. I didn't think she liked me all that much or trusted me for that matter. Thankfully, traffic was light in the middle of the afternoon. As he drove he decided he would just spend the rest of the afternoon at home. But that would put him farther behind, he reminded himself. Life seemed to be interfering lately with his business and campaign and responsibilities were piling up. How did other men handle parenting, marriage and a demanding job? They most likely did the same thing he would, go back to work after dinner.

"Great susgetty," Rick told Julie as she cleared the dishes. Their dinner of spaghetti and meatballs brought to mind happier days spent with Kathy. "What did you want to talk about that we couldn't discuss this morning."

Julie sat down with two mugs of steaming coffee and some chocolate chip cookies. *Lord, give me the right words*, she prayed silently. "It's about Kathy and the final hearing that's coming up."

"David said it shouldn't be anything complicated as long as the Warners aren't going to pull something on us," Rick offered.

"Well, what the Warners do is not important to me. I've prayed and done a lot of thinking about all that has happened. I keep coming back to the same thing. Kathy wasn't ours to keep, legally or morally. Anyway, not the way we went about it. . .I went about it. You didn't feel it was right from the start."

"That's not true," Rick jumped in quickly, taking her hand in his. "At least not once we started making the arrangements. The family we built has been so beautiful."

"Has been. . .was," Julie emphasized. "What are we now? A family of five. Two mothers, two fathers and one very confused little girl. I love Kathy with all my heart. I always will. But, we can't continue to pull this child apart. She needs to bond with one set of parents not two. I'm afraid she will end up hating us all and have no sense of family and the love and security it gives. No amount of therapy is going to provide that. I think we need to let the Warners have Kathy on a permanent basis."

"Listen to what you're saying!" Rick jumped up from the table wincing from the sudden movement. He paced and ran his hand through his hair. "I can't believe you'd suggest this. After all we've been through. . ."

"After all Kathy's been through. It's Kathy I'm trying to think of here. She never asked for all this pain. Fighting the Warners for custody will only bring more confusion and anger, and we can't even be sure we would win. Certainly continuing like we are, with joint custody, is not going to work and Kathy will be the one it destroys. We need to put her first."

"I am thinking of her. How will she feel if we desert her? You think Sebrena can give her the kind of love she needs? What kind of a mother has an affair, tries to abort her own child and deserts the children she does have just to pursue her own interests and desires. Come on, Julie, get serious. I didn't know you were the kind to bail out when the going got rough."

"Do you think this has been an easy decision? You think I just got tired and gave up? Do you think I don't love Kathy or care about what happens to her?" Julie could feel her voice rising with each sentence. "You get serious, Rick. Just why do you feel it's so important to continue this custody agreement? Kathy's not a possession to be fought over. She's a little girl who needs to feel secure and loved. Why can't you see that?"

"I don't believe you." Rick stormed out the door and a moment later, Julie heard the tires of the car kick up the loose gravel in the driveway.

He's not supposed to be driving yet, she thought. Numbed and defeated, she crossed her arms on the table and laid her head down gently. The tears refused to come to comfort the agony. She sat alone in the middle of a silent and empty kitchen.

Wynne knelt beside Kathy's delicate form as she slept peacefully thanks to the mild sedative the pediatrician had given them. She seemed so fragile. He reached out and brushed some stray curls from her soft cheeks. He wished he could be a real father to her. He could feel the love growing for her within himself. But, after the emergency doctor's visit today, he struggled over the decisions that were ahead.

"Mr. Warner," Dr. Thomas had said, "I don't believe there is anything physically wrong that is causing the pain in Kathy's stomach at this point. I think it is just a reaction to her outburst this afternoon at school. I'm going to give you a few of these mild sedatives. She just needs one. That should relax her enough for her to get some sleep. If she still seems overly anxious tomorrow, you can try one more in the morning. I don't want anyone to rely on them to control behavior, however. Kathy is in need of some therapy to help her deal with the constant change in her life. I don't understand how the court system can allow this kind of a decision to be made. It will be taking a toll on her physically soon. She is already bordering on anemia."

"Anemia? How do you know that?"

"Mrs. Sierra was concerned and had me do some blood work." Dr. Thomas flipped through Kathy's file and pulled out the results of the blood test. He flipped the page around to show Wynne. "You see, this is where the normal level of iron should be for a female child her age and this is where Kathy's is. If she doesn't start eating better, we are going to have to put her on a supplement."

Wynne's face reddened as his eyes scanned the report. There was more interesting information here than the borderline anemia. Especially interesting to Wynne.

"Mr. Warner, you and your wife need to do everything you can to help this child cope. I've stressed that to the Sierras as well. The four of you need to work together."

"Yes, we've talked about therapy for all of us. Mr. Sierra's accident put that on hold, but I think we will be ready to begin soon. Thank you for your help, doctor." Wynne shook hands and walked out to the waiting room to retrieve Kathy. His face was still flushed and he could feel the heat in his cheeks.

Kathy stirred in her sleep and Wynne tucked the covers around her. Barnaby and Wilbur looked on from their corner of the bed next to Kathy's pillow, dispassionate observers to the gentle act of love before them.

A light snow dusted the grass over the grave of James Michael Boston I. Lovingly, Michael laid the red carnations mixed with Christmas greens at the base of the headstone as his mother had requested. It had comforted some of the turmoil within him to visit with his mother.

"Michael," Mom had said. "I never realized how much you blamed yourself all these years. I thought you had worked past the guilt you felt as a little boy."

"I thought I had too," he replied sipping his hot chocolate. Kathy's face came to mind. Maybe it was the hot chocolate connection that had set him off.

His mother always made it for him to soothe the rough spots. Hot chocolate gave you plenty of time to talk while the marshmallow melted and the hot liquid cooled. "Seeing that little girl agonizing over her father brought it all back again. I not only made my life miserable by causing Dad's death, but I made you a widow besides."

"You did no such thing. You didn't cause Dad's death and no one has ever blamed you. I hope you realize that. The weather and that old creek did him in. That, and the fact that he always thought that truck could corner like an Indy car. He knew he'd hurt you when he told you he was leaving us. When you lit out of here on Dusty, he took after you as much out of guilt as anything else. Dusty and you would have gotten wet but you two would have been O.K. He just wanted to comfort you, to make everything all right, when he knew it wouldn't possibly be all right again. He made his own choices. You didn't do anything more than react to the frightening prospect of having to be shared by a mom and dad who wouldn't be living together. It tore you apart." She sipped her hot chocolate.

"I may be a widow," she continued, "but I've not been lonely. I have friends and a wonderful son of whom I am so extremely proud." Michael could not speak. He just allowed his mother to embrace him and hold him. There was such security and love in a mother's hug.

"Now," she said. "On your way home, I'd like you to stop by the church cemetery and leave these for me." She handed him the bouquet of flowers. "My arthritis tells me I need to stay in. Must be a change in the weather coming. Anyway, I'd like you to do that for me if you would."

She was one smart lady, his Mom. She knew he needed this time here, with his father. He stooped down and trailed a finger in the snow that was beginning to stick. "I'm so sorry, Dad. I didn't mean to have you end up like this. I was just a stupid kid. Forgive me."

He lifted his face to the falling snow letting the flakes meld with his tears. A surge of pain went through him. He rose. A cold breeze cooled his hot face. Can I forgive myself, he wondered, as he turned to walk away. There was another child he knew who was hurting. One who was caught in circumstances she didn't understand either. There was one small thing he could do to avoid adding more pain to her life.

Sebrena discovered herself humming as she sorted through the size eight suits on the rack. She would need a power suit. One that would give her the confidence she needed to face the challenge before her tomorrow. After she had dropped a rather drowsy Kathy off at school, she drove straight to the mall. While she waited for the stores to open, she did a little "mall walking" and window shopping, being careful not to stop abruptly when another mall walker was behind her. She had collided with one before. One mishap was lesson enough.

Once the gates of her favorite store opened, it didn't take long before she had her arms full of possibilities.

"Would you like to try those on?" the sales lady asked.

"Of course," Sebrena answered, relieved that the woman had finally seen fit to take the heavy load of suits she was holding.

In the fitting room, she found the zippers didn't want to work easily. She tried sucking in her stomach and holding her breath. How could she have gained weight so quickly? The thought of going to a size ten now was unacceptable. She didn't need to feel fat tomorrow. She had another six and a half months to feel fat. I'll just have to get a body shaper, she resolved. Choosing the deep teal suit with the tailored cut, she proudly carried her prize to the car, glancing at her watch to be sure she was still on time for her manicure and hair appointments. It would be hard to refuse her requests in court tomorrow. She would be very impressive and certainly the better choice over Julie as Kathy's mother. She would make Wynne so proud of her.

Nineteen

Frozen Marshmallows

The chairs in Judge Belmonte's chambers afforded no comfort to any of the participants in the case before her. Helen looked at the anxious faces. Her judicial face cracked slightly, and she looked down at her notes to avoid anyone seeing her sympathetic expression and interpreting it as a sign of prejudice in their favor. Actually, she longed for a little prejudice in this case. Something that would allow her to make the right decision. There were no answers yet and here were four parents and a child waiting for a wise and fair decision from her. She cleared her throat, took a deep breath and raised her head.

"I have read the briefs outlining your arguments in this case, gentlemen." Helen peered over her glasses at the two lawyers before her. "Are there any other arguments to be heard at this time?" Helen looked around the room. Sebrena sat stiff and businesslike in her teal suit, a little pale under her meticulous makeup but indomitable. Wynne was studying his shoes, a little out of character for a politician whose eye contact with voters was usually impeccable. Rick and Julie were clutching each other's hands and tears were evident on their faces. David, the Sierras' lawyer and good friend, eyes glistening, was the first to speak.

"Judge Belmonte, if I may?" His voice almost cracked with emotion. "Mrs. Sierra would like to address the court. She has something to tell you that will have a great bearing on this case."

"Of course," Helen said, folding her hands and turning to Julie whose tears now flowed freely. "Please proceed, Mrs. Sierra."

"I. . .I. . ." Julie couldn't get started and sat for a moment trying to gain composure. From the back of the room, Ray moved toward her with a welcome glass of water. She smiled her thanks and sipped. "I have done a lot of thinking and soul searching these past few weeks. When I first saw Kathy in the delivery room and realized she was alive and knew that her mother had wished it to be otherwise, I felt it was God's answer to our prayers for a family. You see, Rick and I cannot have children of our own. I was blinded by my desire to be a mother and I talked Rick into helping me make it possible by going through the process of a fraudulent adoption. I was wrong, legally and morally." She stopped to take another sip of water. The room was stone quiet.

"I have loved Kathy in a way I never would have known a mother could love. It is a love that cuts deeply now because I know what I must do. Kathy cannot survive being split in two between our families. It's taking a toll on her physically, and we can see that wonderful spirit of hers dying a little bit each day. I didn't fight to save her life in the beginning just to become a part of destroying it now. She needs the stability and security of one home, one family, one set of parents. I know the Warners will love her and they have much to offer as parents. I have to. . .I need to. . .to. . .give Kathy to them and trust that God has shown me the right way for Kathy's sake."

Rick put his arm around his wife who was sobbing quietly now. "I agree with my wife," he said. "I know Wynne will be a good father to Kathy." That was all he could say. His mouth went dry.

Sebrena was elated. She gave Wynne an exuberant hug in triumph. She reached out and grabbed their lawyer's hand and shook it emphatically. She looked like she had just discovered she was the guest of honor at a surprise birthday party.

"Oh, Wynne, isn't this wonderful," Sebrena beamed. "We won't have to pursue this in the courts any longer. Kathy is ours."

"Hold on Sebrena," Wynne's expression cut into her celebration. "This isn't right. I can't do this."

"What do you mean you can't do this? This is what we've been fighting for. This is what we've spent all these weeks preparing for. Don't you want your daughter?"

"To begin with, she's not my daughter. I saw the results of her blood test the other day in Dr. Thomas' office." Sebrena had difficulty getting her mouth to stay closed. It hung wide open as her face reddened and clashed terribly with the color of her new suit.

"Your honor," Wynne said turning to Helen who had been quietly listening with great interest. "I see no reason to upset the family environment that the Sierras have established with Kathy. For six years they have been the only family she has known; the only parents she has known. My wife and I are soon to be blessed with another child. Something I had thought impossible, but I have learned much through my new association with Rick Sierra. With God, nothing is impossible. I think Kathy should stay with the Sierras and let them legally adopt her. Sebrena will be willing to sign those papers, officially this time. But, I would ask the Sierras to find it in their hearts to include an aunt and uncle in their family. I've come to love that little girl too."

Again the room was devoid of sound. A passing siren seemed to jolt everyone back to reality. Sebrena seethed. Give up my rights? Sign adoption papers? Let go of everything I've accomplished and planned with Kathy? I don't think so.

"You seem a little upset by what your husband has told us, Mrs. Warner," Helen said bringing life back into the room. "Do you have something you wish to say?"

Sebrena sat straight in her chair, composing herself to begin to speak. Wynne quickly leaned over to Ed Kaplan and whispered in his ear. Ed immediately interjected, "Your honor, would it be possible for us to have a few moments for Mr. and Mrs. Warner to speak privately?"

"Of course. We'll take a ten minute break," Helen said. Sebrena slouched back in her chair, knowing she had missed her opportunity. "The Warners may use the library around the corner. Ray, will you show them please?" Ray led them out and the others filed out into the hall to wait.

"What do you make of all this?" David asked Rick.

"I'd say it's the most wonderful answer to prayer I've seen in a long time."

"Me, too," Julie said. "I didn't understand what God was doing when He asked me to give Kathy over to Him."

"I didn't mean Kathy exactly, although that is wonderful too. I'm talking about Wynne. Did you know that he prayed with Pastor Simon in the hospital cafeteria to let Jesus into his life? This is just more evidence of his decision. That was why I finally agreed to what you were doing today, Julie. I knew that Kathy would have a father who was looking to God for direction in his life. I never guessed it would have worked out this way though. What do you think about them becoming Aunt Sebrena and Uncle Wynne?"

"I guess that's all right. I don't know if I trust Sebrena, though."

"I think we can trust Wynne. And, I think it's the fair and loving thing to do for Kathy, too. Maybe someday she will be able to sort this all out better if she's known her biological mother as well. Besides, she's going to have a little brother or sister. We can't deny her that relationship or meeting her other siblings, Harry's children."

"You're right and you're sweet and I love you." Julie and Rick were studying each other deeply.

"O.K. that's enough you two. Our ten minutes are almost up and you're in a public place." David grinned. "Get your drink of water, or whatever, and then it's back to finishing the work in there."

Wynne kept reminding Sebrena to keep her voice down. They might be in a closed room, but he was sure that their voices would drift into the hall if they got too loud.

"What in the world were you thinking in there? I thought we had agreed on what we were doing about Kathy?" Sebrena ranted on. "I'm not giving up my rights to my own child. I thought you cared about her too. Don't you care about me? How do you think I feel being made a fool of in there? I thought you loved me."

"I do love you Sebrena," Wynne protested. "And, I love that little girl too. She's the one who is making me look forward to having our own baby. I know I can be a father. And with God's help, I can be a good one."

"What is all this God stuff all of a sudden? Did you get religion on me? What are you going to do, be another Harry?"

"No, I'm nothing like Harry and you know it. And, no, I didn't get religion. I got something better. I found faith in a Person who can help me through the rest of my life and beyond. When we have more time, I'll explain it to you. I'm not Harry, and I don't expect to become anything like him. Unless you want to involve Harry in your life again, you'd better decide that the Sierras can have Kathy. Otherwise, we will have to contact Harry and ascertain that he is Kathy's biological father before I will agree to legally adopt Kathy. And, then, you'd have to get Harry to sign over his rights. Do you think he'd do that?"

"Harry's not Kathy's father." Sebrena's eyes betrayed her lie.

"It doesn't matter. She's not mine and that is the plan of action I will proceed with if you don't agree to sign the adoption papers for the Sierras. I love you Sebrena. I want us to have this baby and a clear conscience that Kathy will be able to grow up whole and loved as much as our child will. I want to be a good father to our baby and a good husband to you. Can't you understand all that?"

"No." She turned away from him holding her temples. Panic was making her heart race and her head spin. She didn't want to lose Wynne but she hated giving in. "I'll sign the papers but only because I don't want to have to deal with Harry again. And, so help me, if you turn into a religious idiot like he did, I'll be out the door in a flash. That's my plan of action." She grabbed her purse and rushed from the room before he could answer.

Looking at Sebrena, Julie could understand where Kathy had gotten her pout. She had a moment of sympathy for her until she reminded herself that this was the woman who had almost killed Kathy. Still, a moment of sympathy was more than she'd had in the past. Maybe her attitude could change.

"When I first gave my interim order," began Judge Belmonte after she was assured that Sebrena was willing to participate in Wynne's proposal, "I felt that those who cared most about the welfare of this child would somehow work this out. You see, Solomon once faced a similar problem of two women trying to claim the same child. When the sword was drawn to divide the child in two, the child's real mother came forward to give up her child so that it could live. I feel right in awarding custody to Julie and Rick Sierra. I trust you gentleman of the bar will be able to draw up the correct documents and make this a legal adoption this time." Helen emphasized legal as she looked from one lawyer to the other.

"I will not order visitation rights for the Warners but, I strongly suggest you follow through on some sort of arrangement that will allow Kathy her opportunity to know the rest of her biological family. May God bless you all. This hearing is adjourned."

Sebrena immediately bolted from the room. Wynne looked in her direction for a moment but turned to Rick to shake his hand.

"I'm sorry for the heartache my wife has caused. I treasure the friendship we have found and I hope it will continue," Wynne said.

"I'm sure it will. We'll be seeing each other at church each week. That's a great place for friendship to grow." Rick looked through the door to Sebrena pacing in the hallway. "Is Sebrena all right? Maybe you need to go after her."

"I think Sebrena will need a little time to get past her pride. With this new baby on the way she'll have something else to focus her attention on. Things will be a little difficult for a while, but I'm expecting my friends to pray for us." He looked from Rick to Julie. Julie nodded hesitantly, not sure about this new Wynne that stood before her.

"Let's go get our daughter," Rick said putting his arm around Julie's shoulder. They walked out into the bright light of a beautiful day and paused to take it in. The heavy snow had made the bushes look like they were adorned with giant frozen marshmallows. The whiteness was so pure it was blinding. Rick breathed deeply. "A fresh clean snow for a fresh clean start on the rest of our lives."

Ray tried to give some organization to Helen's desk by retrieving the files and law books she no longer needed. Helen looked up at him over the top of her reading glasses.

"Uh huh. Out with it," she said.

"What?" replied Ray.

"You got something to say."

"Well, I was just wondering if I could borrow your extra 'law' book over there. If I'm ever going to be as good as you at this law thing, I'm going to need the extra help too."

Helen beamed as she turned to retrieve her Bible and handed it to Ray. "The best parts are marked. Keep it as long as you need to." Ray nodded, tucked it under his arm with the rest of the things he had gathered, and quietly left Helen to finish her work for the day.

Michael Boston watched as the Sierras and Warners exited the courthouse. Sebrena seemed to be the only one troubled. Wynne turned in his direction and paused for a moment. "Thanks again," he called out to him with a wave and hurried on to catch up with Sebrena.

Rick and Julie stopped. Rick extended his hand to Michael. "We really appreciate what you did to keep this out of the papers. I know it must have cost you greatly in your job."

"Not a problem. As soon as I convinced my boss I was a total idiot with no sources and no facts, he pulled the story. Then, I redeemed myself by coming up with the inside story of the missing county funds that showed up in one of our commissioners bank accounts. The facts and sources were inscrutable and, once again, I am the boss' pet. Just take care of that little girl. She has a special spot in my heart."

"We will. We have full custody with a legal adoption to follow. It'll be a wonderful Christmas. We'd invite you for some coffee, but we're on our way to pick up our daughter at school."

"Thanks, but I'm going out to my Mom's. If feels like a hot chocolate and marshmallow day and she makes the best. See ya around." He walked to his car. Yessir, Michael smiled as he looked at the bushes full of snow, a hot chocolate and marshmallow day if ever there was one.

AGMV
MARQUIS

Québec, Canada
1999